The Dirty Anthology

I0459587

Cover image licensed by Shutterstock/ © sakkmesterke
Cover design by LJ Anderson/ Mayhem Cover Creations

Editors
Vanessa Bridges – PREMA
Marti Lynch
N. Isabelle Blanco

Publication Date: July 15th 2015
ISBN–13: 978-0692481868
ISBN–10: 0692481869
Genre: FICTION/Romance/Erotica

TABLE OF CONTENTS

ELENA M. REYES

DIRTY
WORDS

How do you SEDUCE a woman
you've never met?
You DON'T You just TAKE

Dirty Words

Copyright © Elena M. Reyes

Cover image licensed by 123rf.com/ ©CuraPhotography
Cover design by N. Isabelle Blanco/ MaE Cover Designs

Editors
Marti Lynch

Publication Date: July 15th 2015
Genre: FICTION/Romance/Erotica
Copyright © 2015 Elena M. Reyes
All rights reserved

One

My computer screen pinged inside the quiet space of my small trailer, and a shiver of excitement ran up my spine. The hours today had been brutal, long, and I was tired.

Cranky.

Fucking horny.

Reaching over, I pulled my laptop next to me on the small couch and opened the browser. I knew who it was. Not one motherfucking doubt in my mind. It was her. *My* girl. The woman who had, unbeknownst to her, consumed every goddamned minute of my days and nights.

Swiping my finger across the mouse pad, I opened my Facebook account—the one no one knew I kept—and smiled. Every day, at that time, she would send me the same greeting.

A simple hello.

Lucia: Hey babe!

What a dangerous greeting. Calling me that term of endearment when all I wanted—fucking yearned for—was a taste of her skin. For her to writhe beneath me while I took what her body would willingly give.

DevA: I'm up. Tired, but seeing your smiling face makes it all better.

1

And wasn't that the truth; I was rock hard as I stared at her profile picture, my palm pushing down against my engorged flesh to alleviate some of the pain she'd created. Conjuring dirty thoughts of her, I released my cock and stroked my hands downward once.

Lucia: You're too sweet!

Yeah, that's me. One sweet motherfucker.

A bead of liquid seeped out from my tip, and my finger swiped across my slit to catch it—used it on my next downward stroke as lubrication.

"Fuck, yeah," I grunted, tightening the hold I had on my cock while opening her pictures. There was one album I loved more than all the others. All her. No friends or family on the beach. Selfies taken of different body parts: her legs, chest…those swollen, bee-stung lips that caused me to push my hips up and fuck my hand.

I fucking abused myself for her. In her name.

DevA: Can't wait to meet face to face. Only a few days left!

There, that should fucking hold her until I finished. My strokes became faster, angrier as I continued to flip through each picture. There's nothing sexier to me than a woman with ink.

Lucia: You are coming, right?

"Fuck, yes." My finger hovered over the screen. Over the picture of her tiny rabbit tattoo barely peeking out from beneath her bikini bottoms. "I'm going to fucking come all over that spot, you hot little…fuck!" I roared as spurt after spurt of hot come fell from my tip and onto my lower stomach.

Lucia: You there?

"I don't give a fuck what you believe in, but you better pray hard. I'm going to fucking destroy you as you have done me. Not one single inch of you will remember any man before me."

DevA: I'm here and baby girl, God himself couldn't stop me from coming to see you.

From coming for you.

2

Dirty

It had been exactly one year to the day since I fell for the words my girl created. A year where I'd spent numerous hours contemplating ways to make her mine. Three hundred and sixty-five days consumed by every book she wrote. With each line my need and hunger grew, my devotion running so deep that I'd lost my goddamned head over her.

Rationality was a novelty I no longer concerned myself with.

She always claimed to have the best inspirations while taking a bath or shower. Was it because she was thinking of me? Was she picturing us together under the hot stream of water? She was a fan, after all.

It was *my* face that my girl watched on the movie screen, and later confessed to being aroused by. I remember re-reading that one post on her wall over and over again. Discovering the effect I had on her was a high unlike any other.

I made her heart stutter.

I made her knees weak.

I caused the wetness to pool between her thighs.

Did she see those images as vividly as I did? Lucia had to have. No one could write such descriptive scenes without putting themselves within their words. My favorite, though, had to be the one time she had me fuck my counterpart in the shower.

Fuck, do I remember that scene:

"Jack, please," Lesley begged as I continued to assault her neck with kisses, biting her hard enough to leave the imprint of my teeth embedded in her skin. I wanted—no, needed, to mark her as my own. The fucking world had to accept that she was taken. "Baby, I need you," she whimpered, "need to feel you inside me. Goddamned delicious stretch and fullness only you can…oh, fuck!" Lesley hissed out as my long and calloused fingers found

her drenched, bare lips. I'd begun a slow rhythm of in and out, my palm coming in contact with her engorged clit and rubbing twice before pulling away.

I was the one making the beautiful woman in my arms cry out in ecstasy one minute, and out in anger the next.

According to her, I was responsible for all the dirty thoughts and words that led to the ruin of her favorite panties. They were my favorites now, as well. Lacy boy shorts had ruined me for all other types. My head was filled with images of those round mounds barely covered by the flimsy fabric. How it molded onto her skin and rode high as she walked.

I wanted to tear them off with my teeth.

I'd pull them down while my tongue would come out to taste every inch of skin my mouth uncovered. I wondered what would hit my tongue as I lay between her parted thighs and lapped at her core.

She'd taste amazing too. Like an erotic mixture of fruits. Delicious.

"Don't tease me, baby. Fuck me. Make me yours." Lesley slammed her hands on the tiled wall while I toyed with her. Broke her down. I wanted her to bend to my will, become insane with lust. When I was through with her, she'd only see me. Feel me. Want me.

Every other male before, and even those stupid enough to attempt in the future, would seem insignificant and unworthy in her eyes.

"Please," her crazed voice pled one last time. She was lost to my touch. My mission had been accomplished.

Withdrawing my fingers, I dropped to my knees before her. "Do you want me, baby? No other man but me?"

Those naughty scenes made my long days so much sweeter. They'd tease and torment. Gave my imagination and cock a jump start of their own as I pictured her playing out those scenes with me.

4

Those scintillating visions that drove her to find immediate purchase before her computer; to lay down those words that would entice my soul. They would call out to that inner caveman in me. That nasty and dirty part of me that wanted to reach through this portal and take what was mine for the taking.

Lesley only managed a small nod as she enjoyed the sight of my face between her thighs. My lips were so close to her dripping cunt—ready to show her my appreciation for the magnificent gift she was bestowing upon me.

"Tell me, dammit! Say it's only me you want and desire." I buried my nose between her saturated lips and inhaled. Motherfucking ambrosia. "I will give you everything you want. Make you come so hard...leave you barely hanging on to reality. Tell me, Lesley, and I am motherfucking yours."

It was the end of that chapter that made me react violently, fisting my cock tightly in my hand, and cursing her for torturing me so. For how hard I came as my cock fucked my fist. How the images of her, fresh faced and innocent, smiling down, helped throw me over the edge. It wasn't the hard fuck my cock ached to give her, but it would do.

For now.

Too much time had passed since that fateful day where our lives became intertwined, where they were sealed together without our permission. A desire to have her close intensified with every tick on the clock. This had to change. No more.

Today all that stops.

"She will be mine," I groaned. Lazily, I ran the tip of my finger down the head of my cock, enjoying the soft caress and the tingles it created. It was her face I watched on the screen. Her smile, the same one I'd imagined time and time again, looking up at me while she took me in her mouth. "Your time is up."

Lucia White, as her fans knew her, was an overnight sensation in the literary world. Her looks were deceiving. Beautiful and pure, yet the moment you read her *dirty words*, all that vanished and what lay before you was an alluring nymph. From the very first page she'd entranced me; I was—and still am—fucked.

"God, I want you, baby. Fucking crave your taste on my tongue." Following her every move became the focus of my days while not on set. She had a private and very naughty group for all her fans. It was a sanctuary of sorts, where she would come in and interact with those, like me, who followed her every word as if it were law.

The only difference was that I pleasured myself to those same words.

Exquisitely mine. There was no denying that she'd owned me from the start. I devoured her exotic features like a starving man. Lucia loved to share bits and pieces of her life through photos, and I am not one fucking bit ashamed to admit that I stalked her.

Signings.

Out to dinner.

The latest was of her with friends at a BBQ.

Tight body barely covered by a tube top and a pair of indecently short shorts that made my cock weep in frustration. Her ass looked so round and high as she spiked the volleyball across the net. Whoever took that picture deserved a huge gift from me.

Each picture was more defined then the last; she was surrounded by friends in every shot. All laughing and smiling, having a great fucking time. Some were with men. They looked at her with the same admiration I held.

"Piece of shit asshole doesn't deserve to breathe the same air as you." They were lucky bastards, and I seethed with jealousy. This was especially true for one overgrown, juice-pumping, dimpled smile wearing motherfucker that in one shot had her over his shoulder. Lucia laughed as the playful moment carried on in film.

I saw red.

My girl's happiness was clear to see. Her eyes had brightened and her face was flushed. Those fucking lips of hers were set into an enticing *'O'* shape that made my heart stop, and my dick swell with desire.

All this for him.

And while she looked more beautiful than words could describe, I wanted to kill him. Take those same fingers he'd wrapped around her upper thigh to keep her in place and break them. Lucia shouldn't have let him touch her.

I'd give anything for it to be me that held her like that. To carry her away from those who wanted what was never theirs, and teach her that only I could give her what she needed.

Two

The first time I laid eyes on her beautiful face, the world and all its bullshit faded away. I wasn't ready for her. Not even close. My life—my job—didn't have space for the emotions and other crap relationships seemed to come with. Then again, Lucia never asked.

She barged in to my life and took over my every thought. Every twitch my cock gave was for her.

Most days, it was a game of sorts as my schedule kept me with odd hours. She had a way of popping in and out, greeting her fans, and teasing the fuck out of me with those sensual pictures of her looking all rumpled from sleep. No makeup. Natural and sweet.

Sometimes, I'd be lucky enough to have my phone with me while on the set. I didn't want to miss her quirky post about all the new *'bunnies'* she kept getting hit with. How they would mind fuck her during all hours of the day.

Bunnies. That brought on more racy thoughts than anything else did.

Did she have one?

What color?

Was she a screamer or did she whimper?

I was not a small man by any means, and I craved the feel of her wrapped around me. Stretching her. Making her feel every ridge of my cock against the walls of her pussy as I took out my frustrations—fucking hunger—out on her.

8

Dirty

"What's up with the scowl?" Clara Knowles, one of my closest friends and co-star in my latest project, said while taking a seat next to me. We'd been called down to the makeup trailer thirty minutes ago, and while I was nearly done, she was late. As usual. Nothing out of the norm for her. "You look constipated."

"Too early," I grumbled and took a sip of my lukewarm coffee. It tasted like shit, but with it being so early, I needed the caffeine. Whoever said that movie stars lived the perfect life was full of it. Three a.m. wake-up calls sucked, no matter whom the fuck you were. "Keep quiet and let them tame the hot mess you are."

"Kiss it," she deadpanned and then proceeded to ignore me, focusing instead on the item in her lap. Her ever faithful e-reader, turned on, and with the latest craze within the female population on display. Fucking horny women and their books.

Her eyes were glued to the screen, devouring each line while fidgeting in her seat. What the fuck?

I was curious and leaned toward her. "What're you reading?"

"Huh?" she answered, yet her eyes remained on the device. Clara was far into the story, more than halfway, but what caught my attention was her flushed face, the labored breaths she took in, and how she bit into her cheek.

"The trailer's on fire," I yelled out and got nothing. Not a damn thing. "There's a spider on your shirt." Not even a glance my way. My hand reached out to pull the reader away. Wrong move.

"Don't," Clara growled before slapping my hand with force. It hurt. Stung.

Holding my hand up to my chest, I glared at her. "Let me see."

"Fine," she hissed while jabbing me in the chest with one of her long acrylic nails. "But lose my page, and I kick your ass!"

"Fuck this. Keep it." Was she for real? What a bitch.

"Don't be such a baby. Read." Clara pushed the small tablet into my hands; she eyed me like a hawk, flinching as my finger stroked the page. This was the crap I got for trying with her. My mood all week had been foul due to our over-packed schedule. I'd holed myself up in my trailer, avoiding my co-stars and crew the moment they called a break for the night.

This had been the first time in days that I'd put in any effort.

"Fuck you, Clara," I snapped, pushing the tablet back into her hands. It was time to leave; I was more than done with her. Standing from my chair, I made a move to toss my coffee and leave, when her hand on my arm stopped me. "Don't."

"I'm sorry, Devin. Please, just read it." Best friend or not, she was being a bitch. However, I cared for the girl, and that saved her from the biting words that sat on my tongue. My glare didn't deter her in the least; instead, she smiled and pulled me down to sit. "I think you might need this more than I do. Maybe, it'll even help take the stick, firmly implanted in your ass, out. Bring back the chilled guy I signed up to do this movie with."

I wanted to rant—knock her little ass out of the chair she sat in— but how could I do that to her when we'd been friends for a few years now? She'd always been my solid, my sister, essentially. Even if our jobs made us act differently, she would always be family to me.

"You're being an asshole, but I'll bite. What's it about?"

"Erotica," she simply stated, an annoyed expression marring her features as I raised a brow. She seemed upset that the word "erotica" meant nothing to me. What did she expect? I lived on set most days and was usually too exhausted to breathe, let alone read or watch TV. Clara sat there, shaking her head at me in disappointment. "Unbelievable."

Wait a minute. Was she talking about porn? My interest was definitely piqued.

"Okay, let's try this one more time." Annoyance with a slight hint of excitement dripped from my tone. *"What's this 'erotica' that has you acting like a raging lunatic?"*

"Are you serious? You don't know what it is?" Much to her displeasure, I shook my head no. This only began a thirty-minute tirade over what this special genre was and just how important it had become in the movement to release women from their sexual jails.

I had two words by the end.

"Give me."

That night after a long and grueling day on the set, I stumbled into the small confines of my portable home and grabbed my tablet from the couch. I was physically exhausted, yet my mind couldn't stop thinking about the book Clara was reading earlier. About the woman who wrote it.

My mind had been made up hours ago; I needed more. More filthy words. More of her.

Opening my Amazon account, I entered her name in the search bar and found the very first picture of her.

"Fuck." The very air inside my lungs had caused me to choke, to fall back on the sofa, and stare at Lucia. The simple picture was by no means scandalous or crude. It was her simple beauty on display while wearing an innocent light yellow sundress, hair blowing in the wind, while she smiled at the camera. *"She's motherfucking perfection,"* I whispered low while running a single finger down her face.

Nothing could've prepared me for the raw desire that coursed through me in that moment.

Cock hard and balls heavy, I struggled with the sudden urge to possess her that overwhelmed me. No, it was an insane lust and hunger so strong that for a moment I struggled to breathe, a dire need to covet her that caused me to ache from head to toe.

I wanted her.

Within minutes, I'd bought every single book she'd ever written.

11

It was with those first few paragraphs that Lucia White won me over. She'd caught my attention without lifting a single muscle.

In her book, the hero was a mobster with a wicked temper, highly possessive personality, and a desire to tame the heroine that I began to relate to. The counterpart was insanely gorgeous, but instead of the typical blonde locks most authors used to describe their female leads, she made her a saucy brunette. No weakling. She had more bite than he did and wasn't afraid to make him see as much.

It was a change. A nice change, if I was being honest.

With each new sentence, my cock leaked and ached for some release. Images came together. Her way of describing the heroine slowly morphed into my ultimate wet dream. Long legs and an ass that was high and tight. Curvaceous in all the right places; with the way she characterized her, my imagination flew and erotic desires grew. I could see it vividly, those legs on her stunning body, my hands grabbing her ass as I plowed into her. Her juices running down my cock, soaking us both.

How she would pull me in closer with each thrust.

Lucia's words seemed to fly right off the pages and morph into my darkest of desires. The way she described her scenes made me curious about the woman who wrote them. A need to search out this woman grew. I needed to know everything about her. Likes and dislikes; how she liked her coffee in the mornings and what turned her on.

I became obsessed.

Abused my cock at night in her name.

Three

My dilemma was this:

The profession I'd chosen ruled my life. Every second of every goddamned day was planned—scheduled, without any input from me. Movie shoots, interviews, red carpets…I always seemed to be too far away from her and on location.

It made things difficult, yet I never gave up.

Wouldn't.

There was something about her that pulled me in; it was a foreign feeling at first, but now I craved it. The lust morphed into something much deeper with every interaction of ours. For once, I felt normal. Not a celebrity or a sought-after bachelor, just a man interested in making a woman his by any means necessary.

So many times I asked myself how I could approach Lucia, when one day I was here, and the next I was gone? In reality, it would be all too easy if I were a normal Joe. After all, the woman lived down the street from me.

Just a few houses down.

"Son of a bitch." My assistant, Jim, hissed through his teeth while his eyes watched a tiny figure running down the street. We'd been standing outside by one of my SUVs ready to depart and head downtown for a photo shoot, when his reaction caught my attention. "Who the hell is that?"

*Every goddamned head turned to follow the woman's form.
What I saw both pissed me off and made me hard all at once. I'd
know that face anywhere.*

Surprised would be putting it mildly the first time I caught a
glimpse of her in person, running without a care in the world in the
world's tiniest pair of bright yellow shorts. The tip of her ass
cheeks just barely peeked out, the flesh round and tight, and my
mouth watered at the sight.

I wanted to bite her, embed my teeth into the succulent flesh.

*"Fuck," I murmured under my breath, watching as my
obsession passed us by. As if she'd heard me, Lucia turned to look
my way as the last syllable passed through my lips. The smirk on
her tiny lips made me smile and a bead of liquid roll down my
cock. "Beautiful bitch."*

*She was temptation of the worst kind and seemed oblivious to the
dangers that lurked near her. For once, I wished that I wasn't
wearing the obligatory baseball cap and shades. That I wasn't
being blocked from her direct line of sight by the two idiots
drooling in front of me.*

My eyes traveled upward and admired her toned midsection, on
display by a simple black sports bra up top. Two mounds, fucking
perky and excited, greeted my line of sight. There was no
mistaking her hardened nipples as they pushed against the top's
material. *Fuck.*

*"I'm moving in," one of my bodyguards declared. He was new
and young. Cocky and immature. My angry eyes flashed toward
him, but he paid me no mind as his eyes were still watching,
coveting what was mine. "Are all your neighbors that hot?"*

They whistled, and I vibrated with pure, red-hot anger.

For as much as I cursed her for existing so out of my reach, I
realized how close—how easy it would be to bump into her and
strike up conversation. Break the ice. Get her familiarized with my
presence, my touch. Enamor her and make her realize how good
I'd be to her...for her.

14

"Shut the fuck up," I snarled and shoved past them, determined to reach Lucia and take her away from their prying eyes. Her body was mine, and I didn't share.

"What did we do?" Jim asked, his face showing concern over my anger and reaction. "You've never had a problem before when we—"

"Shut it and get in the fuckin' car, Jim. She's off limits to everyone, and I don't want to hear another goddamned word about it." They followed my instructions, looking at me with worry-filled faces before getting into the car. Assholes knew better than to piss me off.

When it came to her, everyone was dispensable.

Since that day, I kept an eye out for her when home. Even while away, I kept up with her through our online friendship and the few cameras I'd placed around the front of my property.

Insatiable.

The need grew with each day to be closer, to show up on her doorstep, and offer her the kind of hard—passionate love, most women only read and fantasized about. Make her see past the Hollywood bullshit and desire the simple man I truly was.

Would I ever be anything more than Devin Andrews, the actor, to Lucia? The man she daydreamed of while writing her erotic novels. The same man who fucked his hand in order to maintain some semblance of control when it came to her.

Especially since her pussy lived just down the street from me.

It never mattered in the grand scheme of things, though; I'd make her fall in love with me. Use every trick in the goddamned book if that's what it came to. It was my mission to put a claim on her. No matter what I would have to do—kidnap, lie, or cheat—it would all end the same.

Her body pinned beneath mine, begging me for more of my fingers, tongue…my cock.

"Soon, baby." Her face looked back at me from across the screen of my laptop. Inside my empty production trailer, I immersed myself in her presence. She was running again, down my street. Just like the last two times, Lucia paused outside my properties gate and smiled. Hand on hip she stood, her tanned, lithe body pushing, taunting me with every curve my lips yearned to taste.

She was smiling while perusing the small rosebush I had my gardener put in for her. They were her favorite flowers. All white, with just the smallest hint of a blush in the center. They'd gone in as soon as she mentioned receiving a beautiful bouquet from her parents for her birthday.

"God-motherfucking-damn," I grunted in appreciation of the view before me. Lucia was leaning forward, giving me a close-up of her face and chest. "So beautiful." Her skin glistened with sweat; she was flushed and wearing a small mischievous smile on her face. Those fucking perky tits she loved to display looked delectable inside the ridiculously small sports bra she wore.

With the hand not controlling the camera angles, I cupped my balls and gave a tug. It felt good, but nowhere near good enough to get me to come.

Enough to take the pressure off, because the next time I came, it would be inside my sweet girl's pussy.

"Wonder who lives here?" Lucia whispered low, her chest close to the small hidden lens I'd placed there just for this purpose. I was hoping the flowers would draw her in. "House's always empty, yet has an immaculate garden."

Turning around, she took a few steps away from the outside bush and searched around for something.

"I swear to God, baby…" The sight of her ass so close, right fucking there, made me whimper out in pain and tug harshly on my engorged flesh. Yoga pants had suddenly become the bane of my existence. Another step forward and the flesh jiggled just the tiniest of bits. Once, twice, I pumped my cock in time with each step closer she took, and then released. "I'm going to enjoy coming all over those cheeks…spread them wide apart and paint that tight little hole with my very essence."

16

Right, then left—across the street and back toward the driveway, Lucia searched for something but came up empty. Shrugging, she turned back to face me and walked over with determination written all over her face.

"They won't miss one," she argued with herself before grabbing a single long-stem rose and taking it from the bush. I'd let her take every flower if she smiled like that every time. "I'll bake them some cookies to make up for the theft."

With that, she turned around and sashayed that sweet body of hers down the driveway and out of my sight. I had to smile at her audacity; I had a little kleptomaniac on my hands. I'd make her pay for her offense; a kiss to the tip of my dick and maybe a lick down to my balls would appease me.

Sitting back, I closed my laptop and then my eyes for a moment. "Soon can't come fast enough. I'm going to enjoy you, baby. Every inch."

A sudden knock on the door pulled me from my thoughts. I was ready for this last day of shooting to be over, needed to get out of here and go after my girl.

"Open up, fucker," Clara yelled, the harsh sound reverberating throughout every square inch of my sad excuse of a temporary home. "They need us on set, and quite frankly, I'm not in the mood to end the day at three in the morning...again!"

"Hold on, *bitch*." Of course I mumbled the last part. I wasn't about to piss off the woman I would be fake fucking within the next hour. I loved my cock too much to put him in such a dangerous position. It wouldn't be the first time she kneed me.

"Heard that!" Of course she would. It would be just my luck. "Come on," Clara whined next, "I have a date and don't want to postpone. I'd never do that to you. Don't you want me to be happy?"

Gotta love a good dose of guilt trip.

Nevertheless, in a sense she was right. The faster we started, the sooner I'd be on my way.

17

"Give me five, babe. I'll meet you in makeup." With one more harsh knock on the door, she stomped off and left me alone to my thoughts. As of yesterday, my plan had been put in motion. This little show had just solidified the end of my bachelor days.

All work-related appointments, schedules, or meetings had been postponed. I was following her to an intimate signing in Miami. I'd bide my time. Watching—waiting, never too far away, until the night she was expected to show up for a special VIP event.

An event orchestrated by me with the sole purpose of getting her alone. She would be so close all night inside that packed club. At my mercy.

"You have no idea the kind of trouble your smut filled books have gotten you into. That ass is mine the moment I have you within my grasp. Pray, baby. Pray for help."

Four

It was too much.

Not enough.

And absolute perfection all at once.

I couldn't put her books down. Each word was the sweetest of tortures. If I had a minute to spare during the day, I'd be reading her creations. Yearning and hungry for the more her characters found in each other. The passion that ignited within me at every touch—kiss.

More than once, I saw myself as the hero in her books. It was so easy to envision the way her breath would hitch as I pressed my body against hers. How she would tremble if I kissed my way up her neck and toward her mouth, taking possession of what fucking belonged to me.

It was with those first few lines that Clara pushed me to read, that I became a fan. *Her* biggest motherfucking fan. It was as I devoured every word, every book, that the plans began to formulate in my head. There was never a choice for me; she'd taken that away without any clue as to what she'd done. I had to meet the woman that ignited such primal responses from me.

Months of torture, of seeing her from afar, drove me insane. My desperation grew, and I yearned to ravish her with each interaction online. With each line she wrote. Tonight all that stopped—ceased.

Now was the time to act.

I'd make myself known to her and take that which belonged to me.

Grabbing my phone from the seat beside me, I pulled up the club's information and pressed dial. It rang two times before my dear friend—and accomplice—answered.

"Hello," Clifton, the owner, spoke with a cheery tone. I'd known this fucker for a few years now, he owned a few other bars around the U.S., and they all catered to the rich and trashy. I'd met him through an ex co-star that loved the atmosphere and the attention she garnered the moment she stepped through the door. He was manning the bar that night and struck up conversation. We'd been friends ever since. "Are you in town?"

"Yeah, I just picked up the rental. Thanks for handling that, by the way, but couldn't you have picked out something normal? This flashy, bright orange Charger has everyone looking my way."

"You're in Miami, slick. That *is* normal around here." Motherfucker knew I hated that nickname, and his laughter told me as much. Pulling the car out of the rental's lot, I joined the crazy traffic of the city and merged onto the I-95 expressway heading toward the beaches.

"Fuck you," I deadpanned.

"You're not my type," Clifton reiterated with amusement coloring his tone. "Plus, I like my men wild and Latino. You, sir, are neither."

"Again, fuck you."

"Devin, I like you, bro, but—"

"Shut it," I growled low. Now was not the time for games. I needed him to focus and make sure everything was taken care of. That my plan wouldn't be hindered by anyone's stupidity. "Are we set up?" Looking through my side mirror, I made my way over to the last lane on the left and pressed the accelerator. With traffic lightening up the further we got from the airport, I enjoyed the speed.

It handled like a dream—fast and smooth. I was buying one of these the moment I got back home.

"I should be insulted that you're even asking," Clifton huffed out. "Everything's been set up since ten this morning, right down to the special bottles of liquor, hors d'oeuvres, and the booth you wanted close to hers. Not visible by their party, but you'll have the perfect view."

"And Antonio?" Taking the next exit, I drove toward Collins Ave. and my hotel. The same hotel I'd booked for my girl, her room next to mine.

"Done. The reservation's made, and he was very happy to help. Her group of fans will be treated like royalty tonight, and your favorite bottle of tequila and dishes have been promised to make this the perfect evening. Relax. Everything has been taken care of."

Lucia had a love affair with the south-of-the-border cuisine and always managed to find a restaurant or hole-in-the-wall joint in her travels. This would please her, and that was all that mattered. Her joy was my aphrodisiac.

Pulling the car into the hotel's entrance, I parked in the reserved section and got out. It was midday and the Miami sunshine was beating down on me with force. A few beads of sweat rolled down my brow.

Wiping them away, I popped the trunk open and pulled out my carry-on. There was no need for more; clothing wasn't a priority here. Getting her naked was.

"Thanks, asshole." I smiled into the phone at his laughter. That was one of the things I liked about Clifton—he never took shit too serious. He gave as well as he got.

"My pleasure, ass face." With that, he hung up, and I walked straight to the reception desk. Lucia was due to arrive within the next two hours, and I wanted to be inside my room and away from her line of sight.

She'd see me soon enough.

21

Dirty

My nerves were shot while I waited and paced the length of my room. Knowing that she was so close, yet so far, was torture. She was here with just a mere fucking wall separating us. I could hear her moving around, more than likely walking around in next to nothing.

Or she could be headed toward the shower. *Fuck.*

These thoughts of my Lucia were driving me to the point of no return. If I wasn't careful, I'd unleash myself upon her before the night had even begun. My ears could faintly hear music—an upbeat rhythm coming from the direction her room was in.

The music Lucia had playing was loud and harsh. Drums and congas could be heard from within her room, carrying over into mine. I walked over to the wall that separated us and pressed my ear tightly against it, hoping to catch a small wisp of her voice.

Anything to hold me over until tonight.

She sang slightly off key, her imperfections making her all the more endearing in my eyes. My face stayed plastered against that wall for the remainder of the song and then the next. My breathing came out in short pants as my mind began to conjure up images of my beautiful girl dancing in nothing but her underwear.

Envisioning those two perky, slightly larger-than-a-handful tits jiggling as she moved around the room in a very naughty way. Gyrating provocatively.

Or, maybe she'd be bent over her bags by the bed, rummaging through her luggage for something tempting to wear. Would it be short or see-through? Tight?

My cock was straining against the zipper of my pants as my hips pushed against the wall. I was desperate to alleviate just a tiny bit of the discomfort my girl had created. Then it got worse. So much fucking worse.

22

The sound of the shower being turned on pushed me over the edge of sanity. I couldn't take it any longer, and I palmed my cock. It swelled. It hurt. I found myself lowering the zipper and letting my dick out.

Her shower door made a small squeak as she opened it; we were so close. Just a motherfucking piece of drywall and plaster separated us. I could hear the water hitting the shower walls and floor.

Then she fucked up.

Almost cost me to lose all coherent thought and break down the barrier between us. She let out a deep groan of pleasure a moment later, and I lost my composure.

"Jesus Christ," I grunted in agony and banged my head against the wall.

"What the hell? Someone there?" *Fuck, she heard that,* I mentally chastised myself. It wasn't time yet. No, not yet.

Then the water shut off.

"Hello?"

It returned a minute or two later. I took my cock in hand, my wrist twisting with every upward stroke, while I swiped my thumb across the head on the descent. It was so easy to imagine myself in there with her.

Just like her story, I would come in from behind in her bedroom. My large hands encircling her tiny waist, pulling her back to my front while rubbing my dick against the swell of her ass.

"I need you," I groaned against her soft skin. "Can I have you, baby?"

She trembled in my arms as I whispered these words against the nape of her neck. "Please," she whimpered, her tiny hands reaching back and taking a hold of my cock. Lucia squeezed hard enough to make my knees momentarily weaken—for my eyes to roll into the back of my head. Up and down her hand went, tugging on my engorged flesh. Each pass met with a thrust of my own.

I was setting a slightly harsh pace. "God, you're huge—strong, yet silky in my hands. Can I taste you?" she moaned out as my hand reached around and cupped her supple breast.

Kneading the flesh roughly, I plucked her nipples into stiffened peaks. Teased them until they were both sensitive and she was left panting for more.

"On your knees," I ordered and flicked each nipple one last time. However, before I let her turn around and lower her body, I wanted to show her just who was in charge of our play. First, I needed to wrap her long, silken hair in my hands and take control of her head.

Control her movements.

Jerking her neck back, I caused her lips to become level with my own. So tempting. Juicy.

I devoured.

My kiss was brutal.

In a way, I wanted to punish her for making me want her so badly, for turning my world upside down and making me forget who I was before she entered it. My tongue invaded her mouth roughly, and I claimed every inch. Probed, worshiped, and marked.

I wanted to permanently brand my essence within her, as she had already marked me with hers.

Her tongue was soft, gentle against my more demanding one. I began to slow the intensity and pulled away. Lucia didn't like this and informed me with a glorious pout on her swollen lips. I couldn't help myself and nipped her bottom one. This earned me another pout and while cute, I needed to correct that behavior.

I smacked her ass once, just hard enough to make her hiss in pain.

It was my show.

My rules.

"None of that, baby. Get down on your knees and open wide. Service me." She complied and lowered herself before me, eyes

wide and innocent while she watched me stroke my cock before tapping her lips. "Open."

My pre-come left a string of gloss over the plumpness of her lower lip.

"Mmmm," she hummed as my pre-come covered her lips and her tongue snuck out for a taste.

"Fuck, so sexy." I growled low. "Open up, baby, and don't fucking move." I slid the swollen head of my cock over her lips, letting the warmth of her breath wash over my dick. It sent shivers down my spine. Gently, I moved the head in and out from between her lips while the tight grip I had on her hair kept her in place.

"Fuck, you're perfect," I hissed out in absolute pleasure.

She pushed against my hold, moving her tongue around the tip and over the slit that poured my essence into her mouth. The hand not holding her silky strands reached out and pinched her nipple hard.

"Shit!" Lucia yelped, and then let out the sexiest groan known to man.

She likes it rough, *I mused and smacked the sensitive tip one more time; her thighs became glossy.*

"You like that, don't you?" I stated; it wasn't a fucking question. She opened her mouth, the reply sitting on her tongue, but I was having none of that and pushed my cock in until I hit the back of her throat.

My girl was a trooper; she choked and gasped for air but didn't pull back. Instead, her tiny hands found purchase on my ass and pulled me in closer.

With both hands now imbedded in her hair, I held her head still and fucked that pretty mouth of hers. The sounds of her gagging only served to make me harder. Tears began to form in her eyes with each intrusion; my fingers caressed her face, letting her see that my love for her was still there.

"Fuck, your mouth feels so good," I spat from between clenched teeth as her little tongue swiped over my swollen head. *"Jesus, just like that. Lick the underside, baby, yes... oh, fuck."*

"Fuck!" *she screamed suddenly, and for a second it was real. Better than any fantasy I'd ever had.*

"That's right, baby. Moan my name," I grunted before pulling her off and up. My hands pulled her right leg over my elbow, opening her up. I slipped inside her warm, tight heat before she could catch her next breath. *"So motherfucking good."* My control slipped, and I fucked her with wild abandon. Hips slapping against the flesh of her ass, my arms held her in place while my lips bit into her neck, marking her for all to see. *"Mine."*

"Yours," she screamed. *"Goddamned yours."*

It was that tone of euphoric elation that threw me over the edge. My head banged against the wall as I tried to catch my breath. Never had I come so much in my life. Spurt after spurt left my body, causing my knees to feel weak and my arms to tire, but it was all worth it. *My eyes looked down; a stream of my come ran down the wall and onto the carpeted floor.*

Next time, it would be our combined juices that flowed out her pussy.

A beautiful sight.

Five

"Fuck," I heard her hiss out, and I pressed my ear once more against the wall. She was moaning. It was real. "Please, don't stop." I saw red. Any trace of my recent release vanished with that thought.

Was my girl in there with another? Fuck and no.

"Devin," she whimpered, followed by the sound of a hand slapping against a wall. The red haze disappeared just as soon as it came; my smile grew. I was proud. You couldn't pay me enough to remove the smug grin of my face. "Oh fuck me, Devin."

My girl was on the other side of that very wall, pleasuring herself to thoughts of me. Using my image to make herself come. Perfect.

The water was turned off, and I stood in place, arms braced on the wall, holding my trembling body up. Pure fucking fervor burned through my veins; I wanted her. Needed to feel the heat of her skin on mine, enveloping me.

"*Soon,*" I whispered out low and backed away. "You better be ready for me." It took everything, every ounce of sheer will to pull myself away and start to get ready. Looking down, I found my dried come on the carpet and shook my head while smiling. Before this weekend was through, our combined juices would be found over every flat surface of this room.

It would smell like us. Like perfection.

27

My shower was quick. In and out. I needed to be set for her departure as I would be following shortly after. With sweaty palms, I paced the floor inside my rented four walls. It was only a matter of time now until I had her.

The next time I came, it would be inside her pussy—she would be drenched in me.

"Shit, I'm so late," I heard my girl grumble exactly an hour to the minute after I pushed off the come-stained wall. "Fuck. Devin and his cock…I shouldn't have watched his last movie on the plane ride down." The distinct sound of Lucia's heels as she closed her door and strode past mine became faint the farther away she got. I was barely able to catch a small glimpse of her figure as she cat walked down the hall.

Come-and-fuck-me boots. That's all I could make out of her through the small peephole in my door. These were the kind you wanted your woman to wear as you fucked her. They spelled trouble. A little pain. And a lot of pleasure.

"Bad girl." My whispered words were ignored by the stunning beauty a few feet away. She never turned my way while I closed the door behind me and walked past her. Her smell caused me to pause for the shortest of seconds. She smelled of innocent sin, the kind the good Lord above couldn't with good conscience punish you for; my reactions to the woman were out of my hands.

Lucia paid me no mind while I opened the door leading to the stairs and stood just inside the doorway, nor while I watched her slim form. She was so close to danger and completely oblivious.

The elevator dinged, and my girl huffed. "Come on!" She'd been pressing the down button incessantly, lacking patience; another thing we held in common. Lucia entered the elevator, and I looked down at the watch on my wrist—we were on schedule. My timing had to be just right as I needed to head down without being caught or mauled by *my* own fans.

The moment I was inside my car, I called Clifton. He answered after two rings in his usual jovial way.

"Dude, this will be epic…the place will be packed, but we have everything ready for you. You owe me—" All this was said in rapid succession, almost too fast for me to follow.

I laughed hard. "Breathe."

"But, Devin," he whined out, and I had to put a stop to him. If I let him get too excited, there would be no reining him in tonight. I'd be stuck babysitting an overemotional gay man and not fucking my girl. Not happening.

Bypassing his inane chatter, I spoke. "I'm on my way. Stop, breathe…tell someone to give you a strong shot and relax."

"You suck."

"No, that's what you do. I like to eat pussy." This made him snort and then let out a huge breath. "Better?"

"Yeah. Get off the phone and see your girl." Didn't have to tell me twice.

Once at the restaurant, I parked and entered through the back door. Walked through the large kitchen and thanked the staff as I passed by them.

The owner was waiting for me right by the waiter's entrance with a smile. "Welcome to Antonio's, Mr. Andrews. We are very happy to have you here tonight and help you in any way we can."

"Is she here?" Extending my hand out for him to shake, he took it and the extra few hundred dollars I passed him for all his troubles.

"Yes, sir." Antonio nodded enthusiastically. "She's having a few complimentary drinks by the bar while the group waits for their table to be ready. We were just waiting on your arrival, Mr. Andrews."

Nodding, I clamped my hand on his shoulder, squeezed, and walked through the staff's door and into the main dining room. That's when I saw her, just across from me at the bar sipping on a cocktail and laughing with her head thrown back.

"Fucking beautiful." And it was the truth, something every other man in this restaurant noticed while they admired her. Her face.

Her laughter. Or that motherfucking ass of hers that I yearned to spank. To see the print of my hand adorn those succulent cheeks while she rode me in reverse cowgirl.

No one paid me any attention while I walked across the room and sat down the bar from her. Not in the clothing I had on. I blended in well with the patrons here tonight, and it pleased me. Made me feel normal for once.

Dressed in a simple pair of jeans, polo, and a baseball cap, I was invisible. Even to her.

It wasn't as if I were stalking her, I just wanted to make sure my girl was being treated right. That she was having a good time and not being approached by the sea of men who seemed to naturally flock to her. Her beauty turned heads no matter where she went.

Dinner was sensational to say the least—well, at least my personal show was. Being close enough to witness the way her plump lips caressed the fork after each bite of her food was a beautiful sight. My eyes had an undisturbed view of her heaving chest in the low cut, almost indecent halter she wore tonight.

So close was I, that my ears were within distance to hear the moan of pleasure that passed her lips. My cock was both tortured and thankful.

She was the most alluring creature, and it wasn't just my eyes that realized this. More than once, I had to glare or growl out a warning to the idiots who attempted to approach. See, my girl was positioned at a corner table, two down from my booth. To get to her, you had to bypass me, and those that tried were dissuaded fast from their intentions.

My career be damned when it came to taking care of what was mine.

I would fuck any one of them up; of that there was no doubt.

The girls had a blast as they ate and got to know each other on a one-on-one basis. I could hear the murmurings, squeals, and laughter as they all discussed her latest book and crush on me.

"Jesus, the things I would do to that boy," one said as she fanned herself, earning a laugh from the bunch and a blush from my one and only. "Suck him so good."

"Oh my God," another one of her fans squealed. This woman I knew; she was from Arizona and an admin on her page. "Look at Lucia's blush. What's going through that head of yours? Spill, missy."

"It's just, this um... fuck. Okay, there's this scene that I've had in my head lately. All I see is Devin taking me hard and fast. No romance or soft touches. A motherfucking claiming, and it's driving me insane." Everyone at the table laughed and ribbed her some more in hopes she would spill.

"Is that all?" the one that started with the offer to blow me asked. "You usually have so much going on in that head of yours."

"No," Lucia grumbled before taking a long sip from her drink. "There's one more bunny. A bit naughtier, and different from anything I've written before. It's consuming me."

"Don't leave us like that!" some woman yelled out much to my girl's embarrassment.

"Fine," she huffed with a smile. "And this is all I will say on the matter. Devin is older in this one, a much older doctor than my supposed eighteen years. Yes, my ass is young in this fantasy. He's a dominant, and falls for the town female version of a troublemaker. She's about to turn eighteen, and he waited until then to pounce and correct her behavior."

A chorus of *"fuck,"* and *"yes, please"* rang throughout the table. The women around her all giggled and began to talk about chains and whips. A little disturbing, but I'd love to tie Lucia to my bed. Maybe use a few toys to torture her for making me become this crazed asshole for her.

They discussed this new idea until it was time to go; the bunch was surprised, yet elated when told that a patron had paid for their entire meal.

Of course, Lucia protested, but it was a done deal at that point. No way of getting around it. Her beautiful eyes scanned the room hoping to find the gracious guest's eyes, but as she searched, they happened to land on mine.

Reality slipped.

I could see the recognition flash through her expressive eyes. Disguised or not, she knew who I was and was seconds away from saying so. It was just my luck that a friend pulled on her arm, her eyes diverted, and I took that as my cue to leave.

Leaving through the busy dining room was easy. Everyone's eyes were too busy watching the live band playing to notice the celebrity escaping. Once outside, I made my way over to the driver I'd hired for the night and gave him the exact instructions of what I wanted.

"Deliver them to the club precisely at ten, and not a minute earlier. It's important, and if you fuck this up, I won't be happy."

Nodding, he extended his hand out and took the envelope with his pay and generous tip. "Of course, sir. Ten on the dot, and I'll make sure they get there safe and happy. Will I be waiting outside after?"

"One of them will be returning with me, but the others will need to be returned to the hotel. Keep close to the front. It's been arranged for you to park there without any issues from the owners."

"Understood."

"Good." Nodding, I turned around and made my way over to my bright orange rental. Opening the door, I slipped inside quickly and tilted the seat back just a bit. My girl should be coming through those doors any minute now, and I shouldn't be seen.

Lucia didn't disappoint.

No sooner had I climbed inside when she walked right by me. Her eyes were looking everywhere. *That's right, baby, search for me. See only me.*

She walked next to me and then stopped, her eyes trying to get a look inside the car I was sitting in. Lucia tilted her head to the side and through squinted eyes searched all around for the something she'd seen. No dice. Too bad for her my windows were tinted all black and impossible to see through at night.

"Come on, Miss White…it's time to get our party on," one of her readers declared. It was followed by choruses of *"hell, yeah"* and *"bring on the liquor"* from others.

They all piled into the awaiting van, and you could see most of them already wearing the effects of the alcohol consumed with dinner. The entire group, including my girl, danced in their seats as they drove down to Club Mansion. I followed them just a few cars back and laughed at their antics. It was cute.

People in the cars around them, through heavy traffic, were amazed by the rowdy bunch and cheered them on.

Only in Miami, I tell you.

Six

The music was thumping as I entered the club. From my understanding, the group was already being seated in the upper level VIP lounge, and was well on their way to enjoying their first of many complimentary bottles of tequila.

The latest club banger from a popular male Cuban artist had just begun to play, and almost every person in the room walked towards the dance floor. Bodies swayed—hips grinding and lips singing the catchy tune, that now had become an instant favorite of mine.

She was on the floor when I approached—in the middle to be exact—with quite a large fan base watching her every sway. Never had I seen a pair of hips move so enticingly to a beat. It was almost as if the conga and drum beat flowed through her veins.

She was the envy of all women in the room and a temptation to all men.

No one saw me as I made my way across the room and stood behind her. Mere feet away by the bathrooms, I hid and watched my girl dance. Witnessed her be propositioned and turn every motherfucker down.

Good girl.

Lucia stayed on that floor for nearly an hour straight, only stopping because she was signaled over by her friend from

Arizona. She held Lucia's phone in her hands; it'd been ringing nonstop for the past five minutes. All calls had come from me.

It was time.

"Your phone's vibrating, chicky," she yelled over the loud music. "We were going to ignore it, but it kept ringing. We didn't know if it was an emergency or not."

On your mark.

"Let me see." Lucia opened the screen of her phone and sighed. "It's a friend. She's supposed to make it tonight. Ah shit, she needs me to call her. Fuck, I hope she isn't canceling."

Set.

"Call her; I'm sure she just needs directions." With a nod and her phone tightly gripped in her hands, Lucia walked right into my trap.

Mine.

Her back was to me when I reached her, concentrating on the phone call she was attempting to make—a call that would never be answered. My hands took hold of her tiny waist and pulled her flush against my chest, her back to my front. Her body stiffened and her mouth opened to let out a scream.

"Don't," I whispered against her throat before laying a small tender kiss beneath her ear. "I will release you in a minute, baby, but I won't be letting you go. No screaming. There's no need to be afraid."

"Please, don't hurt me."

"I could never." Another kiss and then a gentle bite on that sensitive area beneath her ear. For someone so afraid, she never attempted to push me away. Instead, she stood there and followed instructions like a good girl.

"Then let me go," she begged, and I smiled. She'd be begging for an entirely different reason soon.

"You captured me with your words, Miss White. Motherfucking ruined me, and I only think it's fair that I return the favor. I'm yours, if you'll have me." My hands released her slowly—now, she fought to move away, but the moment we stood face to face, she stood as still as a statute.

"You," she accused, much to my amusement. "I fucking knew I saw you." Lucia began to pace the small hallway, tiny measured steps, but not once did she venture far. "Motherfucker, am I being Punk'd?"

"No, babe. And yes, it's me."

"Oh fuck me."

"I plan to."

"Oh God...you!" She was in shock, as was to be expected, but at this point the girl literally looked to be well on her way to passing out. That wouldn't do.

My lips crashed onto hers before she could utter another word. Lips, so soft and pliant against mine, battled for dominance. They wrapped themselves around my tongue and began to suck. That action sent sparks of electricity to my already heavy balls.

"Motherfuck." A low growl ripped itself from deep within my chest, and my hands reached down to squeeze her succulent ass. Her sinful body molded itself against my harsher planes. Every inch of her was wrapped around me, rubbing herself against my hardness. "I need you."

My eyes almost rolled into the back of my head.

"Please," she whimpered while I picked her up and wrapped those legs I'd dreamed about around my waist. Her back hit the wall; I used it to hold her top half up while my hands held her hips still. She protested with a weak growl of her own, and then she did the cutest thing in the world:

She bit her lips.

Cute, but not working on me this time, baby.

"Don't fucking move, love." This time I got a glare. "I'm not kidding, Lucia."

She rolled her denim-covered pussy against my cock. "Or else what?"

"Keep that shit up, and I'll fuck you right here, against this wall, for any motherfucker who comes back here to see." She opened her mouth to speak, but one harsh bite from me on her lower lip kept her quiet. "Now, that being said, I'm taking you home with me."

Her groan made every nerve ending in my body tingle. "My friends—"

I ignored her and licked the swollen lip. "I wasn't kidding when I said I was putting a claim on you. One way or the other, I will have you, but I would prefer if you wanted this too."

"But... fuck, that feels good." Her tiny fingers embedded themselves into my hair and pulled. Her hips continued to move, seeking the friction she needed. "We don't know each other, Devin."

My name coming from her lips sounded so sweet.

"We've been friends online for months, sweetheart."

She pulled back to search my eyes for any sign of deceit. "What?"

"I know you hate the dark, and think Friday the 13th movies are traumatizing. You love the ocean and collecting sea shells from the ones you've visited thus far." Her eyes were huge and filled with unshed tears. "Also, I know that when you were eight, you had the biggest crush on a member of a popular boyband we won't mention."

"You're DevA?" she asked, and I nodded with a smirk. "Oh God, how embarrassing." Lucia pushed her face into my neck and hid. The heat from her blush warmed me. She remembered that conversation now through private messages.

"And finally, I also know that you masturbate to thoughts of us as you write. It's that quirky, yet feisty girl that I want to fall in love with."

"This is insane, Devin. I don't know you."

I had to put a stop to this shit right there.

"Yes, you do. Every conversation we've had online was real. Everything we've discussed—from our favorite music, to literature, to the porn sites we frequented—was honest. All of it." A single tear ran down her cheek. "I told you all about my childhood, and the death of my chihuahua Rocky. About my cousins, and their penchant to pick on me because I was the last to hit puberty. You know me, love. Know the real me—not the man in front of a camera, but the dork who loves Guns N' Roses and reads comics."

"Please don't laugh." She giggled while wiping her cheeks. I raised a brow. "I began to think I was a lesbian…"

I choked on my spit. "Come again?"

"Thought I was falling in love with a..." My lips smashed into hers once more.

"Want you, Lucia."

"This is crazy, but God do I want you too, Devin. Have for a long time." I couldn't help but let out a booming laugh at the way this declaration had turned out—we truly were a pair.

We left the club immediately after. She told her friends she was feeling ill. They wanted to leave with her, but after assuring them she just needed to sleep, we were off. We walked out hand in hand toward the private parking area for the club's famous clientele. The moment her eyes landed on my car, she punched my arm.

"Ouch." Violent little thing.

"I had a feeling I was being watched as we passed by."

"I've been watching you all week, baby." Leaning down, I lightly bit her neck and she let out a tiny moan. "I can't wait until I'm buried balls deep inside that sweet pussy of yours."

"You're mean." She pouted while I chuckled and opened the door for her.

"Not when I plan to deliver the moment I have you back in my room."

Dirty

The moment we stepped through the penthouse I had rented for the duration of our stay, I had her pinned against the door with my mouth attached to her flesh.

"Please," she begged while my lips trailed over her collarbones and down toward her chest, following the edge of her barely there shirt with the tip of my tongue. Her chest rose and fell rapidly while I bit into the swells of her breast. Each nip was followed by the soothing caress of my tongue as I worshiped her every pore.

"Take my top off, please. I need to feel you, Devin." Her impatience scorched my veins. She wanted me. "Just take it the fuck off!"

"As you wish," I snarled and ripped the offending halter in two, the sound of splitting fabric only enhancing the erotic moment. My girl arched her back, neck straining as she pushed her breasts toward my face.

"Fuck, you're beautiful," I murmured before taking a stiff peak into my mouth. Her breasts were so soft in my hands, such a contrast to the pebbled flesh I was currently biting, licking, and flicking between kisses.

"Shit!" Lucia hissed, her fingers gripping my hair tight and pulling me closer.

"Like that, do you?" I couldn't help myself; seeing her so lost in the sensations I was creating—it was a boost to my ego and cock.

"Yes." Her hand reached down to unbuckle my belt. *Way ahead of you, sweetheart.* The moment her hand encountered the hard flesh of my cock, her body shivered and her lips opened in a silent '*O.*'

Lucia's eyes snapped up to mine, watching me while stroking my engorged flesh. "So soft…so huge."

"I want you to feel me for days after—every time you walk, you'll feel an ache, a twinge of pain, from how far I've stretched you."

"Please." Her plea came with a harsh tug on my cock; my body trembled in an effort to hold back. There was something I needed to hear come from her lips first.

"Please what, Lucia? Tell me what you want and I'll give it to you."

"Fuck me. Stretch me. Break me." Music to my goddamned ears.

"You shouldn't have said that."

Within seconds, I had her boots, pants, and underwear on my floor. Her lacy pink boy shorts hung from my finger, the saturated fabric enticing me to sniff the drenched spot as her intoxicating scent hit my senses. Drawing the lace toward my nose, I took in a deep inhale and groaned.

Her natural smell was sweet and fruity. My body wanted to cover hers, claim what was mine, and begin to satiate the thirst I'd had for this beauty for quite some time. Instead, I pulled back and enjoyed her natural enchantments. My girl's body was a work of art: pert breasts, flat stomach, yet she had wide hips that led to a bountiful ass that begged to be fucked.

There wasn't a piece of her that wasn't perfect.

My eyes continued their perusal until I hit her pussy. Bare and pink. Swollen lips that were bathed in her essence and a tiny clit that peaked out from between her flushed labia.

My mouth watered.

Seven

"I'm sorry," I apologized before grabbing her thighs forcefully and picking her up. With the wall against her back, I placed each leg over my shoulders and her pussy within my mouth's reach. Right fucking there. She was suspended in the air with nothing other than my hands, and the wall, supporting her weight.

"Oh fuck," she squeaked as I blew warm air over her clit. It twitched and trembled. "Devin, please don't drop me."

"Shut up and let me enjoy," was all I said before I dove in. That first burst of her taste on my tongue made me delirious, hard as steel, and leak. There was no softness in the way I ate her. Licked and sucked the juices she released from her swollen lips. Her taste was addictively sweet, just as I'd always imagined my beauty to be.

"Fuck." I had no idea who screamed it, but at this point I could seriously give a fuck. She ground her lips against by face. Her tiny hands fisted my hair as I devoured her core. My tongue caressed her clit with gentle flicks before I pulled it between my teeth and shook my head from side to side.

She thrashed and filled my mouth with her wetness.

"So fucking sweet," I grunted against her pussy, causing her to pull back and away.

"Sensitive," she whimpered, but I was having none of that and bit her bundle of nerves. She exploded and gushed into my

41

awaiting mouth. Her body jerked hard—spasming without any control as wave after wave of pleasure took over her body.

Lowering her body down as gently as I could into my arms, I nestled her against me and carried her over to the large, king-sized bed. I looked down at her still blissed-out form, our eyes met, and a feeling of complete calmness enveloped me.

This was it.

She was it.

It was in those few moments that I took it all in and began to thank whomever upstairs had bestowed her upon me.

"Falling in love with you will be so easy, Lucia," I reverently declared before sliding into her for the first time. There weren't enough words in the English dictionary to describe how she felt. The tightness—the softness. I'd never experienced this before. Didn't know it could be like this.

Her arms wrapped themselves around my neck and tugged me down toward her awaiting lips. "So easy," she whispered against my mouth. Tears began to roll down her cheeks; I wiped them away with my thumb and kissed every inch of skin I could reach.

It was overwhelming and comforting all at once as our bodies soothed the other. Like a warm blanket of adoration, welcoming us into nirvana as we lost ourselves in the other's embrace.

My hips sped up as her legs wrapped themselves tightly around my waist, the feel of my girls' walls as she stretched and latched onto my girth making me lightheaded. It was indescribable to finally feel her surrounding me. Both heaven and hell all rolled into one.

Lucia was perfect for me, my other half in every sense of the word. I had no doubt in my mind that when my girl was created by the man above, it was with me in mind. She was designed specifically for me.

Everything in this fucked-up world made sense with her in my arms—with her heat enveloping me. We were destined to meet. I was meant to find her as I did, through her words, and fall for the woman behind them.

My girl was supposed to become fascinated with me. Read and watch every movie I had ever made and dream of me at night. To be inspired by me and create the worlds brought on by her fantasies to pull me in. Clara finding her books and introducing me to them was all part of destiny crossing our paths. Of this I had no doubt.

She was my one. Taken from my flesh and molded to fulfill my every need.

"Oh God, please..." she screamed as my hips swiveled against hers, my pelvic bone brushing against her engorged clit with each pass. "Yes!" Fuck, she looked amazing with her head thrown back, eyes closed, and hands fisting the sheets.

"Beautiful," I groaned before placing a quick, yet chaste kiss on her swollen lips. I sat up on my knees and grabbed her hips, pulling them up and off the bed while still impaled on my cock.

The only parts of her still touching the mattress were her shoulders and head. Everything else on her delectable body was now in my power. Bending to my will.

I manipulated her hips, made her ride me as fast, or slow, as I desired. It was making her thrash and scream in agony. Needing to prolong the inevitable, I would slow us down whenever signs of her coming undone were visible.

"Sweetest motherfucking pussy..." I trailed off as she squeezed down on my dick. Hard. My eyes rolled back. "Yeah, baby, fucking ride me."

"Shit!"

My fingers found purchase on her hips and held her still, the stranglehold she had on me making me tremble. Fucking vibrate with the need to break her as she'd so clearly done to me.

Quickly, while she tried to catch her next breath, I flipped us over and slammed back in. My hips met hers in an almost angry pounding; everything was crashing into me and making me emotional. Elated. Crazed. And with a sudden maddening urge to possess and mark like never before.

I fucked her. No other way to describe it but as a good, old-fashioned, fucking. Hair fisted in my hand to hold as reins, the other on her hip or occasionally smacking her ass hard enough to leave my handprint on the succulent globes.

"You are fucking mine. Do you understand that?" She whimpered in answer. That wouldn't do. "I said…" another hard smack landed across the flesh of her right ass cheek "…do you understand?"

"Fuck, yes. Jesus, I'm yours, baby, just make me come." Lucia attempted to throw me off when I didn't comply. I could see her intent to force me onto my back and mount my cock; maybe any other day I would have been all over that shit, but not today.

With both hands on her hips, I yanked her back forcefully and pulled her up to my chest. I was in deeper now, being choked and seconds away from erupting and painting her walls with my essence.

"You want to come?"

"Yes," she begged, while pushing her ass against me in provocation.

"As you wish." I rode her harder than I thought was humanly possible, her ass smacked against my thighs—the force stung, but the reward was worth the red ass prints I now proudly wore.

Her body tensed, back arched into an almost painful shape as her walls locked down. Watching her come and letting go was beautiful.

"Motherfuck," she howled. Every nerve ending in my body felt as if it were a part of hers—I felt her pleasure down to my bones. The moment her first gush of wetness burst through, momentarily forcing my cock out, I began to erupt. Slamming back in, I held still and enjoyed the feel of her juices dribbling down to my balls.

My spurts swirling with her juices were soaking us both, creating a new heady scent that saturated the room in the beauty that was us. She collapsed first with me following a second later, the plushness of the bed welcoming our exhausted limbs.

"That was amazing, Devin," she hoarsely whispered, then turned her face and laid her head over my still erratic heart. "Thank you for making *this* fan's dreams come true."

I think this was the first time I disagreed with her words. They were completely ridiculous. Wrong.

"No, Lucia, it's my deviant dreams that came true the moment I read your books and discovered the beautiful soul that lay beneath each line. You're my equal in every perverted sense of the word. Perfect for me." Her warm body collided with mine, lips grazing my chest in a sweet kiss full of promise and maybe in the future: love.

"So does this mean I get to make all my dirty fantasies a reality? With you?"

"Only me," I stated. No, it was more like a demand.

"I could live with that." She laid a tiny bite over my pulse point; I felt her smile against my skin. "You know, I've always dreamed of having you fuck me in the shower."

"Lucky for you, I'm in the business of making all your desires come true." With that being said, I jumped off and pulled her toward the edge of the bed where I now stood. She giggled and tried to fight me off, but one quick spank to her bottom made her stop. "Get the fuck up and in that bathroom."

"Yes, sir," she sassed and stood up to salute. I had a feeling our fantasies would keep us busy for the rest of our lives. Her naughty side rivaled mine.

I was a lucky bastard indeed.

The End.

About the Author:

Elena M. Reyes was born and raised in Miami, Florida. She is the epitome of a Floridian and if she could live in her beloved flip-flops, she would.

As a small child, she was always intrigued with all forms of art—whether it was dancing to island rhythms, or painting with any medium she could get her hands on. Her first taste of writing came to her during her fifth grade year when her class was prompted to participate in the D. A. R. E. Program and write an essay on what they'd learned.

Her passion for reading over the years has amassed her with hours of pleasure. It wasn't until she stumbled upon fanfiction that her thirst to write overtook her world. She now resides in Central Florida with her husband and son, spending all her downtime letting her creativity flow and letting her characters grow.

He's determined to have her—
she's determined to watch him burn in hell
before that happens...

MAC
Tease

SYSTEMATIC SIEGE:
Provocative Tendencies

Episode #1

Amazon Bestselling Author
N. Isabelle Blanco

Systematic Siege: Provocative Tendencies #1
SSPT SERIES

Copyright © N. Isabelle Blanco

Cover image licensed by 123rf.com/ © George Mayer
Cover design by N. Isabelle Blanco/ MaE Cover Designs

Publication Date: July 15th 2015
Genre: FICTION/Romance/Erotica
Copyright © 2015 N. Isabelle Blanco
All rights reserved

Theme Song:

"Addiction" by Dope

1
PRESENT

The wealthy don't have time to grieve.

It's a lesson my father drilled into my head over and over throughout my life. When my dog died. Again when my grandma died—both of them.

Yeah, he didn't let me grieve the death of his own mother.

If he mourned her, I have no clue. No one does. We never saw any sign. He just went about his business as usual.

He'd been a strict authoritarian, that one. Among other things.

I wonder if all those years he was busy drilling the lesson into my head, he'd known it would one day apply to his own death.

Food for thought, huh?

Well, in case there is such a thing as an afterlife, I want you to know old man, that I learned the lesson very well.

I'm sitting here, at the top floor of the skyscraper you built, in what was once your office—an office that recently got remodeled to better fit my tastes.

And I'm calm. Cool. Collected. So unperturbed by your passing, Father—despite the fact that I caused it—that I'm starting to think something's wrong with me.

Then again, considering the type of man my father was, maybe all of this is perfectly normal. I'm not the only one that isn't aching over his passing. No one seems too broken up about it.

My mother isn't. I don't blame her. She put up with enough crap from that man.

His own brother isn't too sad, either.

So, like I said, maybe I'm normal after all.

"Drew. Are you ready?"

Speak of the Devil.

My uncle Robert stands at the entrance to my office, hand braced on the glass door.

He's been asking me that question ever since we agreed that I would be taking over my father's place as CEO.

My uncle refused the position and I'd had no choice. There are many on the board that would love to drive the whole Drevlow family right out of the company now that my father is gone.

I can't allow that to happen. Can't do that to my mother. She deserves all the comfort and privileges this company affords her. She went through enough being married to my father. I'm not letting her suffer anymore unnecessary bullshit.

And it had been the perfect revenge against my father. The best way to get back at him for what he once did to Lexi's family.

"I'm going to take your place as CEO."

"It's about damn time you smartened up and decided to do the right thing."

So much contempt. Even as he lays in a hospital bed, machines struggling to keep him alive, his feeble heart replaced with a new heart that his body is rejecting. Smiling coldly at the man before me, I lean toward him and whisper, "I'm only taking the position so that one day, when I find Lexi, I can give it to her."

My father's eyes bulge out of his head and his face turns bright red.

"That's right." I nod. "Once I find her, I'm going to make sure a Berkman ends up in charge of your company."

2

I killed my father with that promise. Didn't lay a single finger on him. The last word left my mouth and the rage he felt exploded inside him, his blood pressure skyrocketing and sending him into yet another cardiac arrest.

I killed my father because he believed the conviction in my voice. He knew I'd been serious. That I meant every word.

It's that conviction that brought me to this point—the head of a company I didn't want to run, my feet on a black marble floor, surrounded by glass, steel, and gold accents.

Sitting behind a brand new desk, in a way too-big office, and metaphorically in the shoes of a man I'd come to loathe throughout my life.

For my mother.

And Lexi.

Wherever she is.

The power this company gives me will be enough to help me find her.

I *will* find her.

I can't even think her name without that old, crippling rage squirming inside me.

As I've been forced to do for seven years, I push the memory of her back. Remembering that I'd lost her, *how* it'd all come to pass, is toxic in ways my relationship with my father never was.

Until I can find her, I can't afford to wallow in her.

God I want to. Get lost in the vision. Let the ache consume me. It would be so much easier than this constant battle, always having to fight my own psyche and the way it yearns for her.

I tried that once. Almost lost my fucking mind. The pit I ended up falling into was too deep, darker than anything my human mind could've ever imagined. My self-destruction came close to spilling over into the lives of the few people I loved.

Because I loved her more than I'd ever loved anyone.

More than I loved my own mother.

3

I still feel that way. Time has done nothing but make the emotions more powerful.

Pulling myself out of rock-bottom took a year of rehab. I live with the guilt of that every day. As well as the guilt of everything else.

There's too much at stake for me to even consider drowning my misery out like I did before. I've just inherited immeasurable power. It's time to start using it to get the woman I love back.

Then I can begin making up for everything I allowed to happen to her.

So I stand, button up my dark-gray blazer, and face my uncle. "I'm ready."

2
PRESENT

I was nineteen years old when I graduated from alcohol to drugs. On the exact day that marked the one year anniversary of Lexi's disappearance from my life. My binge only lasted six months; enough time to leave a lasting mark.

It took one car crash and the subsequent realizations that hit me to get my stupid ass to wake up.

I was causing my mother pain. Her teary eyes were the first thing I saw upon awakening in the hospital.

The all-body cast encasing my body was the second.

That's when my next realization slid into place: I would never find Lexi if I ended up killing myself.

Her and my mother's faces got me through the next year of therapy, when I had to wait for my body to heal, and had to relearn how to use my legs properly.

All while battling to break free from a heroin addiction and being forced to face the demons that caused them in therapy.

That's how much that girl came to mean to my pathetic, egocentric, sixteen, seventeen, eighteen . . . and nineteen year old self.

5

I'm lying. She meant that much to me way before.

Since the beginning.

You're not supposed to know what romantic love feels like as a child.

I'm pretty sure I knew.

And that's how much she still means to the twenty-five year old man I've become. The man that's about to use all his resources and break at least five federal laws, if not more, to locate her.

Step one: befriend the new head of the IT department so that she'll make sure all the employees overlook what I plan to do with the systems.

Why am I thinking about this, even when I know I shouldn't allow myself to, at least not until I'm closer to actually implementing the first step of my plan?

The elevator doors I'm standing in front of are a bluish-gray steel that's messing with my head.

Reminding me of blue-gray eyes staring up at me, hazy with pleasure.

A bolt of heat slashes right through my nervous system, igniting my heart.

Ah, fuck. My dick is hard and I'm in an elevator, next to my uncle.

"The new head of our IT department is one of the best, Drew."

Beautiful. My uncle decides to start speaking to my while I struggle to get my body back under control.

Trust me, the last thing you want to hear when your cock is pounding is a relative's voice. Much less your *uncle's* voice.

"Mmhm," I mumble, staring down at the marble floor. I can't keep staring at the steel in front of me.

Not if I want to meet this new super-nerd my uncle hired without my dick standing straight and tall before her face.

Mother of Shit. Even thinking the word "nerd" is too much for me to handle right now.

"We managed to steal her from Menahan Industries," my uncle continues, voice brimming with pride.

Deservedly so. Menahan—that little bastard—is our direct competition. Luring one of his employees away had to have been expensive as hell, not to mention legally complicated.

An impressive feat.

I can't formulate any type of response though.

Big blue-gray eyes, framed by those thick black glasses I'd loved, had locked on mine that night, showing me every emotion I'd caused in her.

Every emotion I'd *owned.*

Her brow had scrunched from the pleasure I gave her, her lips parted, begging me to take them.

To take everything.

"Andrew! Oh . . . you're . . . I'm coming . . . uh!"

Fuck, her cries. As long as I live, I'll never forget them. Those sweet little moans still have the power to make me come harder than any woman ever has, even though they only exist within my memories now.

Lexi came all over my thigh that night.

Then my fingers.

It hadn't been enough. I'd attacked her again later that night, eating her out on the hood of my car, under the stars, and the experience fucked with me on a molecular level. Forcing her thighs open, I'd made her drench my tongue, her walls sucking me in deeper and deeper with each orgasm I gave her.

I still remember every freaking facet of her taste. What it felt like to have her swollen little clit in my mouth.

But she hadn't come all over my dick. There hadn't been a chance.

I lost her the very next morning.

"Andrew? Are you listening to me? Are you alright?"

No, I'm not. Haven't been for so long now that I'm starting to wonder if I ever really was.

7

Do I even have a clue what "normal" feels like?

"I'm fine. Just a lot of my mind."

My uncle nods as we exit the elevator on the lowest floor of the building; where the IT department is located. "It's a lot to take in at once. I know. These introductions are necessary though."

I don't dispute that, because he's right. At this point we've visited every department, made sure everyone has seen the face of their new boss. My uncle has been around much longer than me, obviously, so he's well known.

Feared in his own right.

Respected.

Oddly enough, also well-liked despite all that.

His introducing me to everyone is a strategic business move. I'm the son of a man that wasn't known for having been the best type of human being. If I'm going to keep the board under control, I have to make myself invaluable to the company.

I have to become everything my uncle is, and more. Employee fealty goes a long way to helping a CEO retain their position of power.

But as I follow my uncle down the marble and steel hallway, I'm having a moment of utter weakness. One of many throughout my adult life.

The latch in my mind is busted wide open, the door barely hanging on by its hinges. There is no barrier between my mind and the memories.

One in particular comes on strong. It's the one that kills me the most. The full, amazing, *bitter* recollection of what happened the first night I tasted her.

The night that would lead to my losing her.

The night she'd been mine in every sense but the one that mattered most.

3
7 YEARS AGO

I think Stephen is starting to suspect what I'm really coming to his step-dad's gym for.

Sure, it seems like he's brought into my lie of just wanting to come here and practice on my own. It's not like I haven't done it before. For years, I've found random places—anywhere I can hang my punching bag from—and spent hours going at it by myself.

Practicing my uppercuts, jabs, haymakers, round house kicks. Tearing my body down physically so I won't have to deal with any of the mental shit I've got going on.

Everyone at school sees me as some type of warrior. A prized fighter even though I don't professionally fight.

I never will. My father would kill me if I even mentioned stepping into the ring.

At school, the "official" sport I play is football. After school, Stephen, Barnard, and I practice mixed martial arts. It's our thing. Stephen's uncle owns an MMA studio, and that's where we all hang a lot of the time.

If I'm not practicing on my own, as I said.

My friends know I've got some kind of issues. They don't have the details, but obviously something has to be wrong with me if I insist on spending large periods of time by myself.

9

Yeah, I'm aware. The irony isn't lost on me. I hear the whispers. One of the most popular guys in school is actually a closet loner.

Bite me.

Father pisses me the fuck off on a daily basis. Sometimes two or three times a day.

I rather be by myself when I work through the anger. Pushing my body to the max, exhausting myself, is the only true outlet I have.

Breaking Father's face would be lovely, but mother has already instilled in me how wrong that would look to everyone we knew.

Always keep up appearances and all that.

So when I'd told Stephen I wanted late night access—as in: "Get me the fucking keys"—to his step-dad's gym, he'd seemed to have no problem saying yes.

That was three weeks ago and everything had seemed cool.

Until today. Earlier, when Stephen asked me if I was going to use the gym tonight, I could've sworn I'd seen an odd glint in his eyes.

Maybe it's just my guilt superimposing shit, though. Because I *am* lying to him about why I come to the gym.

I'm sure you've guessed by now that it has nothing to do with working out.

Every night, after ten, I sneak out of my house, drive two miles to the gym, and meet up with a girl.

Not just any girl either.

A girl that used to be my best friend, back when we were kids.

A girl who lost her father and family stability because my father is sometimes the legend of Mephistopheles made manifest.

A girl that lights me up so hard, like nothing else in the world can.

A girl that *isn't* my girlfriend.

This is all so fucked up.

Don't get me wrong. I'm not cheating on my girlfriend with Lexi.

Do I want to?

Hell no. What I really want to do is dump Kaylee so I can be with Lexi. That's what I fucking want.

Can it happen?

Do humans have the ability to magically sprout wings and *fly*?

Apparently, I wasn't born to have anything I want. Fuck my free will, or any possible desires born from it. It's all about what my father wants for me.

He has my entire destiny mapped out.

I approached him last week, letting him know I planned to leave Kaylee.

And why.

I know. Stupid me, right?

His words . . . Man, they made me want to break shit.

"Kaylee is a Whittacker, boy. Clearly, you're as stupid as I always figured you were. You want to leave a Whittacker for a Berkman? Did you forget what I did to her father when he thought he could get in my way? Do I have to get rid of her too? Or are you just doing this to prove to me what a disappointment you truly are?"

Ah. My father. King of the Assholes.

Here's the thing: I'd leave Kaylee any way if Lexi showed me even a hint of interest. Like *that*.

I've seen small glimpses, little things here and there that make me believe . . . If I'm going to go up against my father, make Lexi his target, I need to know for sure.

There can be no doubt.

All I think about is her wanting me back. Being with her. It keeps me up at night, messes with my concentration at school.

A never-ending secret fantasy since the girl started developing into a woman.

I slide the key into the lock, opening the back door of the gym, all the while shaking my head at myself.

11

4
7 YEARS AGO

ANDREW

It's normal that I want Lexi as much as I do, you know? She's always been one of the nerds; no living, breathing guy with a functioning dick gives a fuck.

Lexi chose early on in the sixth grade to alienate herself from the popular kids in school. Back then, we'd called them every infantile name in the book. Nerds. Losers.

I say "we", because thanks to my father's social circle, I'd been drafted into the popular crew the moment I stepped foot in school.

Even back then, Lexi had been adorable. Round, blue-gray eyes. Full pink lips. Those big blond curls falling over her shoulders.

No wonder she grew up into what most guys at school have dubbed "the Destroyer." Adorable isn't the only adjective she can proudly claim. Her style isn't particularly In-Your-Face sexy—something Kaylee and her clique love to tease Lexi about relentlessly—but nothing in the world can hide that type of attractiveness.

It's blatant. Wild. Leaks into every part of her personality, so that just the sound of her breathing leaves you panting in response.

Watching her walk leaves you a throbbing, pre-coming mess.

Hearing her voice keeps you up all night, jacking off back to back, because you can't stop imagining what it'd be like to hear her moan your name.

I'm sure you can guess the real reason Kaylee and all her friends despise Lexi. They know damn well that all the guys at school walk around in a haze of sexual fantasies, all thinking about the one girl that doesn't even try to get their attention.

Nerds, emo-fucks, and jocks alike are ready to prostrate themselves at Lexi's feet, *sans* clothing, if she would so much as smile in their direction.

Anger sparks at the thought. As always. I can't deal with that reality. Hate ruminating on how all the other guys want her as much as I do. That shit drives me crazy in ways even my father can't.

Pushing it all aside, I glance at the purple gift bag I'm holding as I walk into the gym.

It's Lexi's eighteenth birthday today.

I never forgot the day her birthday falls on. Not even after we were separated at ten.

I'm early, so I get busy turning on the lights in the back office. I place my book bag on the side table by the couch. Last second, I decide to hide the gift bag on the floor, behind the couch.

I want to surprise her.

Unzipping my bag, I pull out my advanced computer science textbook. Lexi thinks I'm failing that class.

I'm not.

Yes, I lied to her about that. Don't think I'm not aware that I have more of my father in me than is healthy. Unlike my father, however, I am capable of feeling guilt.

And I do. Every day that she sneaks out of her house to come meet me, because she thinks I'm failing a subject that I'm actually passing.

With honors.

Why did I lie to her?

13

Why does anyone ever lie? Either because they're trying desperately to get out of a situation, or because they want something so bad they're willing to risk that age old threat of eternal hell to get it.

The opportunity presented itself, longing choked the ever-living fuck out of me, and I couldn't fight the impulse to take it.

For years, I'd watched my old friend from afar, missing her. Knowing what my father had done to her family. I'd just wanted to have the right to talk to her again.

When that aforementioned opportunity popped up, no preternatural, Zeus-gifted willpower could have stopped me from taking it.

The door creaks open out in the hall. "Andrew?"

God—Nature—whatever the fuck is out there—what the hell did you do when you allowed that girl to come into existence?

Ungh, that voice. I freeze on the spot, eyes closing. Hating and savoring the heat that drums through my veins, pounding its way straight to my cock.

Her voice is how I imagine an ancient sex goddess' voice would've been. If this is how the ancient Sumerians imagined that Inanna's voice sounded, no wonder man eventually rose up and obliterated her legend.

No female, even a mythical one, should be allowed to have so much control over man.

It's not an exaggeration, either. Every fucker at school goes glossy-eyed whenever Lexi so much as hums near them.

The perfect soft rasp; the epitome of the term "sex voice". Every time she says my name, I die a little more inside.

"Andrew?"

Shit. I need to hear her moan for me—don't care if it ends up being the death of me—and I can't fucking have it.

One day I'm going to snap and take it anyway.

"Andrew, are you here?"

14

I clear my throat, sitting down on the sofa as fast as I can. My text book gets positioned just right, so that it covers my aching hard-on. "Yeah. I'm in here."

Jesus, talk about rasps. My voice is straight up laden with sex.

I clear my throat again.

Three deep breaths, and I convince myself that I'm ready to face her. That, although my dick still throbs to the beat of her name, I'm well on my way to getting my reaction under control.

She stops in front of the door.

My entire world grinds to a halt.

Jesus.

Air . . . Can't breathe . . . Motherfuck, this hurts.

My.

Fucking.

God.

Son of a bitch.

Shit, I think I'm wheezing.

Legs.

Those breasts.

That hair.

The eyes.

Red lips.

Lexi all dolled up—no, fuck that, *sexed*-up.

Like I've never seen her before.

It's the hardest blow of my life.

And, it's the exact moment in time I realize that girl *has* to be mine.

Whatever it takes.

Whatever it ends up costing me.

Mine.

5
7 YEARS AGO

"H—hey," Lexi murmurs softly, shifting from foot to foot.

Probably nervous because I'm staring at her like a brain-dead idiot.

My mind is the complete opposite of dead right now. Thoughts race, flying. Cataloging. Processing every delicious inch of what stands before me.

Lexi usually wears jeans. Button downs. Sensible cardigans. Converses, or boots in the winter.

None of that is in sight right now.

No, she isn't naked. Lord in Heaven, I don't think I'd survive seeing her without clothes.

I'm barely surviving what I'm seeing now.

That bright blue dress hugs everything. Tiny straps wrap around her shoulders, and the low cut, square neckline has a two-inch slit in the middle that clearly shows off her cleavage.

No way she's wearing a bra under there.

Her cute little feet are encased in black flats.

I'd known she had a hot body, but fuck. Me.

That *body*.

I can't fucking deal right now, and her face just makes it all so much worse. My heart pumps like crazy and I tell myself to look away.

I fail.

It's bad.

I eat her up with my eyes. Those big blond curls I'm so fixated with frame her face, her shoulders, falling all the way down her back.

My heart punches hard against my ribcage again, angry at me for denying it what's before me, for subjecting it to the sight of so much beauty.

Her eyes are highlighted by black eyeliner, framed by even darker, thick eyelashes. The look in them tells me that I'm doing it, I'm giving it all away, she can see how much I want her, clear as fucking day.

I can't stop.

The same lips I dream of sucking on, stained by dark red lipstick, become so much more to me.

Those are the lips I breathe for.

The lips I'd kill for.

In the future, I will do wrong, dark, evil things for this girl. To myself and to others.

And those lips will be a big part of the reason why.

A wild, primitive hunger roars inside my gut, demanding its due. "Jesus, you look fucking beautiful," I growl out, too lost in the affect she has on me to even try and hide how I feel right now.

Beastly.

Deranged.

Like I'm two seconds from picking her up and flinging her onto this couch, so I can pin her to it and rub my dick over every inch of her.

"Thank you," she tells me, breathless.

17

That voice hits me like a lick across my cock. I force my body not to move a single fucking muscle, because if it does, it's going to do what it wants to do and head straight to her.

Lexi steps into the office, hands fidgeting.

I'm making her nervous.

Shit, I'm making myself nervous. I have no clue what I'm going to do next, if I'll be able to rein in my impulses. "Why are you dressed like that?"

Not that it's any of my business, but the thought occurs to me that she might be dressed up like that because she's planning on going out.

She looks like a girl would look when heading out on a date.

Fuck that. That shit *is* my business. "Why?" I demand again, ready to jump off the couch and block her way back out.

"I . . . some of my new friends convinced me to celebrate."

I can tell by her expression that she thinks I don't know why she should be celebrating. My mind gets stuck on her mention of "new" friends and I rack my memory for any clue as to who they might be.

Last week, I remember her hanging out with some of the chess crew. She'd been talking in the hallway with two girls . . . and two guys.

Two dorks that had looked like they'd been seconds away from busting a load, just because she stood near them and spoke to them.

Is that who she's going out with?

An eerie stillness falls over me. I have no right to feel jealous over a girl that isn't mine.

Which tells me everything I need to know. This one *is* mine. Or, to be more exact, I am hers.

Shit, I've known that for months now. It's why I went to my father and let him know I'm leaving Kaylee.

For her.

For Lexi.

Fuck my father's consent. I'm doing it. I'm claiming this girl. Because thinking of her going out there, looking that beautiful, being herself, and some other asshole picking her up, making her feel special, *dating* her, makes me violent.

I'm going to have her.

But first, I gotta make sure she's going to be okay about it.

Holding her stare, I let the textbook fall onto the couch next to me and I get to my feet. Slow. My movements echo the stillness that still surrounds me. That unerring, calm certainty that I know heralds something more.

6
7 YEARS AGO

If she reacts to me that way I hope she does, I have no idea exactly how I'm going to respond. All I know for sure is that there won't be anything slow, still, or calm about it.

Lexi blinks behind her glasses, her hands falling to her sides. Her eyes are locked on mine.

Her chest trembles with a shuddering breath.

The muscles of my back ripple with that breath. I clench my fists. My chest tenses.

She does it again, as if somehow feeding off what I feel.

Suddenly, it's too damn hot in here. I rip off my windbreaker, leaving me in only my gray t-shirt.

Lexi's eyes widen, then drop down the length of my body.

Fuck. I'm so ready for her.

Please tell me this means she's ready for me.

I cross the distance between us in four strides, taking my time, each step methodical.

I'm giving her a chance. Letting her see me stalk toward her. What I plan to do when I get there.

That I'm waiting for her to open her mouth and protest.

She doesn't.

And I'm in front of her now, head angled down to stare at her because she's so short compared to me.

She tilts her head back slowly to stare up at me.

Her chest trembles again.

My fingers twitch with the need to grab her, haul her against me. By sheer force of will, I reach up slowly, giving her even more time to pull away.

She'll never know how much it costs me. How hard it is for me to not just grab her like I want.

Like not breathing even though you're suffocating. Like refusing a piece of steak after starving for over a week.

Her throat moves with a swallow, but she doesn't move away. She remains there, still, waiting for me.

Fuck.

I cup her face in my hands.

Her lids flutter but she doesn't let them close, those eyes going cloudy on me in a way I'd only dreamed of before now.

"Lexi . . ." I let my thumbs move across her soft cheeks.

Her lashes flutter again.

Lightning courses through my veins because this is it. This is the reaction I'd hoped for, *prayed* for, the one I knew deep down I was going to fucking get.

All I want to do is eat that juicy mouth of hers, but somehow I keep myself under a tight leash.

One that is quickly loosening, seconds away from breaking.

"Happy birthday," I breath, my vision hazy from the force of my hunger for her.

Her eyes widen.

She thought I forgot. That I didn't know.

I caress her cheeks with my thumbs one more time. "I never forgot," I tell her softly, teeth grinding against each other.

Those pretty cheeks go pink, and her eyes shine with a mixture of confusion, shock, and delight.

That's when I get worried. That glow in her eyes tears through the last of my self control. I waited years for her to talk to me again. To let me back into her life.

It seems like I waited my whole fucking life for her to stare up at me like that, with that little pleased look in her eyes.

Now that I have it, a force rips through me, one more powerful than I anticipated.

I'm meant to put that glow in her eyes.

Me.

I'm meant to be that for her. I know this more than I know my own name right now.

I'm meant to own this woman, every emotion in her, every ounce of her happiness.

Her body.

Holy fuck, *yes*. I'm going to have that body. I'm going crazy just thinking about it, but somehow I keep myself there.

I got my reaction. I can start exploring this attraction between us.

But I can't do what my body wants. I want to fuck her right on the couch behind me. Then I want to fuck her on the side table that's up against the wall.

Lexi isn't that type of girl. Not to me. She deserves for me to date her, make her my girl before I fuck her.

"Thank you." Lexi nuzzles the palm of my hand.

I force myself to let go, because God, I want to fucking eat her and I can't. "I . . . got you something." Turning, I head over to grab the gift bag off the floor.

7
7 YEARS AGO

"You did?"

The surprise in her tone rubs me the wrong way. I resolve to gift her things as often as possible from now on. So that she'll never again be surprised that I got her something.

When I straighten, Lexi is there, behind me, standing in front of the couch. She looks all excited, nervous—delicious in every way that counts.

I sit on the couch, holding the purple bag.

It's her favorite color. Always has been.

Wonder if she picks up on the fact that I still remember that, too.

"Come here." I watch hungrily as she slowly eases down onto the couch next to me. "It isn't anything huge, or crazy. It's something small, actually. I wanted to get you something I knew you would like—"

She cuts off my rambling. "Andrew. Give it to me." Lexi smirks at me and holds out her hand.

It's a sad, sad fact that while I stare at her outstretched hand, the gift bag is the very last thing I want to give her. Well, I do want to give it to her, but first, I want her to hold something else. A part of my body.

And not just the obvious part, either. I'd be happy just having her small hand wrapped around my own.

Ah, shit. That's more than sad. It borders on pathetic. What the hell is this girl turning me into?

Oh, but I know. Don't fucking like it; can't fucking fight it.

"Drew?"

She hasn't called me by that nickname since we were kids.

I go hot at the sound of it. So freaking hot. *Blazing.* The urge to rip off my clothes is ridiculous.

"Here." I hand her the bag and brace my elbows on my knees, my clenched fists hanging in between. *Don't reach for her. Don't touch her.*

For the first time, I honestly hope Lexi isn't a virgin. I'm not going to be able to be gentle with her once I'm in her.

She reaches into the bag. Her brow scrunches when she pulls out the wooden box in it. She turns it around and her eyes widen when she spots the necklace hanging inside, right in front of the Harry Potter logo etched into the small mirror.

Her shocked eyes lock on mine. "Drew," she gasps.

Don't fucking touch her.

I clench my fists harder.

"You got me a time turner?" Her low, tender tone makes her voice sound even sexier.

And makes me feel like I'm the most accomplished motherfucker walking the Earth.

See? Told you. It's my job to put that happy little look on her face and her reaction right now just proved it.

I barely stop myself from puffing out my chest like some cocky loser. "Well, it was either that, or Hermoine's wand," I tell her. "And I saw it hanging out of your bag the other day. So . . . knew you had it."

Lexi opens the box with shaking hands and brings the necklace out. The chain glints in the light. I made sure to get her a custom-

24

made, gold version of the necklace. No way I was getting her the fake shit.

"How did you know I love Harry Potter? Just because you saw the wand?" She doesn't look up at me, eyes still glued on the necklace in her hand.

Which is fine by me, like that she can't see the look on my face when I answer, "No. It's because I pay attention to you. A lot of it."

Our eyes lock again.

"Drew . . . " She stops and swallows heavily.

What does that look in her eyes mean? Damn it, *what*?

"Thank you so much."

I open my mouth to respond—

Lexi leans forward and presses a kiss right against the corner of my lips.

8
PRESENT

My uncle clearing his throat rips the memory from me. I feel the loss of it so acutely that I want to push him into the wall for taking it from me.

He didn't actually take it from me. It's still there, etched into every piece of my mind, lurking. As always. All I need to do is turn my attention to it, just a little, and I'll be overcome again. Transported right back to that night.

I can't. My uncle is standing in front of a set of large doors that lead into the main lab of the applied sciences division; a branch of our IT department.

However, we strictly develope hardware in this part of the department, something only a select few people know right now. We're planning on taking the market by storm.

That explains the need for the handprint and retinal scanner next to the doors.

" 'Drew?" My uncle waves at the scanner. He doesn't bother to ask the question that I once again see in his eyes: *Are you alright?*

I step up to the scanner and place my hand on it, then bend slightly to let it scan my eye next. My uncle has the same level of clearance I have—absolute—but he wants me to get used to doing all this by myself.

Not that small shit like this is difficult, but it was never my intention to take over this company—that is, until the day I realized it'd be the perfect revenge against my father—and I'd made that very clear to everybody after I lost Lexi.

My uncle prides himself on being a better father figure to me than my father was.

He is. Always has been. That's why I let him have his fatherly moments where he gets to show me around and "teach" me everything I need to know.

The doors unlock and we walk inside. I haven't been here in a while and I'm impressed with the set-up now that it's all done. This entire part of the division was completed in less than eight months. Considering the scope and size of it all, and the sheer amount of equipment in here, it's a huge feat.

My uncle nods toward a group of men standing in front of a large LCD.

I follow him over to them, taking in the image on the screen. Python coding stares back at me—one of the main languages in software development.

I don't have enough time to read through all of it but I'm pretty sure the group of men we're approaching are the ones heading the Providence project.

Sure enough. We stop in front of the work station facing the LCD and I spot the large black goggles on top of it.

Rumors leaked late last year that Menahan had begun making their own version of the Oculus Rift, the video gaming goggles currently being developed. The Oculus Rift goggles will allow gamers to virtually step into the worlds of the games they play and visually experience them as if they're inside it.

Menahan, that little bastard, has no interest in the gaming world. He's into informational theft. He disguises it by presenting his "innovations" to the public as regular security software advancements.

But we all know what his clients truly hire him for.

My uncle and I are also very aware who one of Menahan's main targets is going to be.

Us.

That scumbag has a personal vendetta against us.

Against *me*.

That's okay, though. I have an ever bigger one against him.

He's one of the people that hurt Lexi.

He has no fucking idea what's coming to him.

My uncle makes quick work of introducing me to the group of men surrounding the Providence goggles; mainly, Paul Rundlett, the man leading the entire project. "Paul here is working directly with the head of our IT department. He left Menahan when she left and came to us alongside her."

Paul smiles at me, his blue eyes lighting up at the mention of the new head of IT. "I'd follow that girl anywhere and she knows it. Berkman is a bloody genius and working alongside her is a pleasure."

A name. One that isn't even that unique. He could've been talking about anyone.

Don't ask me how I knew he wasn't. I just did.

My veins go ice cold.

My focus becomes engaged on him and only him.

I'm probably staring at him like a goddamned lunatic but I don't care. "What was that name again?"

Paul blinks. "Uh . . . Berkman? She's the main developer on the Providence software now. Did you get a chance to meet Lexi yet?"

The world spins dangerously. I stagger back, feeling like I've just been hit.

And that's when I catch sight of my uncle's wide eyes and the expression on his face.

9
7 YEARS AGO

I've been hit many times in my life. Mentally. Emotionally. I'm no stranger to pain in all its myriad forms, have experienced every level of it from a measly one to a devastating ten.

Lexi's lips linger on my skin for a second longer than they should, the corner of her mouth pressed intimately to the corner of mine.

I hear her surprised inhale when she realizes what she's done. She moves to pull away and it hits me: I've never felt this kind of agony before. Nothing's ever come close.

She can't take this away from me.

I won't let her.

My hand snaps around the back of her neck, stopping her. Her face is mere inches from my own. So beautiful that I just want to nuzzle it.

Later. First, I need those lips back on my skin.

"Andrew?" She stares into my eyes, curious.

I see the hunger in her eyes, the one that almost matches my own.

It's enough. A start. I'll make her burn as much as I do by the time I'm through with her.

I lean in and brush the tip of my nose across hers. "I need your lips, Lexi." She will never know how much.

"A—Andrew . . . we shouldn't."

She's so fucking right.

I pluck the necklace out of her hand and blindly dump it back into the gift bag. "Tell me you don't want me to kiss you," I say, staring right into her eyes.

Those glasses she's wearing look so sexy on her.

Somehow, she's keeping them on while I do her. No matter how rough it gets.

Her hands wrap around my shoulders. "I . . . can't say that."

Exactly the answer I expected.

The one I wanted.

God help us both.

"Baby, I'm going to kiss you," I breathe against her lips.

Her last warning. This is her last chance to say no.

Her eyes slide closed.

Groaning, I fit my lips to hers. My entire body jerks at the first, silky contact.

It's like I waited my entire fucking life to feel those lips. Fuck. How did I ever live without this girl's mouth?

I don't press for more, leaving our lips meshed together, taking every breath that leaves her into myself. My blood has never pounded so brutally through my veins; my dick has never been this hard.

I want her tongue more than I want my next breath, but I won't be able to handle feeling it. Not without pinning her beneath me and taking everything she has to give.

Lexi shudders and my body responds with a shudder of its own.

I give her bottom lip one more peck and move back, ending our kiss. I can't go further. Too many things are roaring in my head. Things I need from her that can't happen right now.

She grabs onto my neck, my jaw, bringing me back to her mouth.

30

Holy shit. I can't resist this.

Her tongue slips inside.

A moan is torn from me, my self-control along with it. I cup her face, my tongue playing wetly with hers.

Lexi. This is fucking Lexi kissing me, and when a small moan leaves her, my entire body reaches a breaking point.

I have to stop kissing her. If I don't, I'm going to fuck her. Right here. I don't even know how far she's gone.

I haven't taken her on a date yet.

She deserves so much better than to be fucked on a couch in the office of a gym.

Lexi latches onto my bottom lip, sucking on it repeatedly. Soothing it with her tongue. Like it's her little play thing.

My pulse explodes everywhere inside me.

"Lexi . . . fuck. Wait," I whisper, too out of breath to speak any louder.

She lets me end our kiss and sits there, panting—eyes heavy-lidded, cheeks pinks, lips swollen from my kisses.

Oh God. My fucking cock hurts so bad. I want her hands on it. *Now.*

Suddenly, she gasps, a horrified expression taking over her face. Her hand flies up, fingertips pressing to the lips I just kissed. "Shit. What did I just do? God. I'm sorry. Why'd I do that? You have a girlfriend!" She shoots off the couch.

10
7 YEARS AGO

I jump up after her.

Lexi paces across the small office space. "Stupid. I'm so stupid. Why would I do something like that?"

I grab her shoulders. "Listen to me. Stop blaming yourself. *I* kissed you."

"Why did you?"

That's a question I definitely shouldn't answer. Not here. Not under these circumstances.

I have no choice. Her big eyes remain on mine, waiting for an answer, and they're both curious and vulnerable.

Us guys? We play with girls. That's what we do. Girls hate us for it, but most are so desperate to have us in their lives that they let us get away with anything. With women being so willing to forgive us, why should we change?

This isn't the first time I've cheated on Kaylee. Hell, no. She knows I have, too. Oh, she was furious when she found out, but she came chasing after *me* when I tried to end it.

But Lexi . . . if she was my girl, I wouldn't play with her, cheat on her.

Shit. I really wouldn't. The thought of hurting her in any way makes me sick.

God help me. I think I love this girl.

Shaken by that revelation—and feeling absolutely fucking stupid because I'm just admitting this now—I cup her face.

Fuck. I hope she can't tell that my hands are trembling.

"I . . . " Have no idea what to tell her without divulging what it is that I really feel for her. Too soon for that. At the very least though, I can go with some honesty. I don't like the idea of her thinking I'm just playing with her. "I like you, Lexi. Have for a while. When I felt your lips . . . I just couldn't stop myself."

Her eyes soften momentarily.

My thumbs twitch on her cheeks, aching to smooth over her skin.

But I won't take more. I refuse. There's things that have to be straightened out first before I can have her mouth again.

A fact that's driven home with her next statement.

"You have a girlfriend." She moves to step back.

Away from me.

I drop my hands to her shoulders, shaking my head. "I'm only with her because my father wanted it."

Her expression darkens at the mention of my father.

I don't blame her. "I'm leaving her. I even told my father. He knows it's you I want."

At that, her face goes pale. "Andrew, your father hates my family."

My father has no real reason to hate her family—but he's always been good at deluding himself like that. He's fucked you over? Easy fix. All he has to do is convince himself that you somehow deserved what you got. It's all your fault. He's just the victim lashing out in the name of retaliation.

He'll go after Lexi and her mother if *I* get in the way of his plans to unite our family with Kaylee's. That's what Lexi's afraid of. She doesn't have to say it out loud; I thought it, too.

I drop my hands to grab hers. "I know, and I'm sorry. I shouldn't have told him why I'm leaving Kaylee. I just—forget it." Pressing my lips together, I stop myself before I can go further, realizing how pointless this is right now.

Until I'm officially single, I can't be completely honest with Lexi. It wouldn't be fair to her.

But she doesn't let it go.

I kind of expected she wouldn't.

"You just what, Andrew?"

She hasn't pulled her hands out of mine, letting me rub my thumbs into her skin, and I take comfort in that.

"Andrew?"

I sigh, giving in. There's no way I can resist telling her the truth. At least part of it. "All I could think about was being single so I could ask you on a date."

She arches her eyebrow, making me smile. "Just to ask me on a date?"

My smile widens. "To start."

Her eyes flicker all over my face, pausing at my mouth.

"And when I start dating you, Lexi, I'm not fucking hiding you from anybody."

Her juicy lips part and my cock throbs painfully for them.

Soon, I'll have those lips all over my naked body. Wrapped around the swollen tip of my dick.

I throb in my jeans again at the thought, my tip slick against my briefs. Tightening my hands around hers, I breathe through the rush of desire, reminding myself that I'm doing the right thing by waiting.

I've never waited for a girl. Never had to. This shit is already proving to be harder than I thought it was going to be. I've never done "right" by a girl. I want to with her. The reminder is the only thing that keeps me steady.

She wiggles her fingers, signaling that she wants me to let her hands go. I do, but it takes a shitload more effort than is normal. Smoothing her hands across my shoulders, Lexi steps closer, looking up at me with those sexy, open, vulnerable eyes that somehow scream at me to *do her.*

My body shoots tights with tension.

"Are you serious right now? Or are you just playing with me?" she asks softly.

I growl under my breath, angry that she would even think I'd do her like that. "Lexi, I want you to listen to me and listen well." Pinching her chin, I make her stare into my eyes. "I've never wanted anything as much as I want you. And I'm damn well prepared to do anything I have to do to have you."

11
7 YEARS AGO

I expected her to react to that comment a million different ways. With disbelief. Anger. Maybe even fear.

Imagine my shock when she steps even closer, pressing every inch of her body against mine.

Heat flares everywhere. Inside my body. Outside it. In the air that crackles with pure electricity around us.

Her thin arms come around my neck and she lays her head on my chest, right above my raging heartbeat. Snuggling into me, she gives me the sweetest hug I've ever been given.

There's nothing sexual about this hug—well, unless you count the fact that I'm hard as freaking steel, and her abs are pressed right against my cock.

I hear what might've been her surprised gasp, but she doesn't pull away. No. She snuggles into me again, her head tucked under my chin in the most adorable way. I wrap my arms around her, returning her hug.

She gives me a happy little sigh.

God, she makes my fucking chest ache.

I duck my head and press my nose to her hair, inhaling her scent.

Her arms tighten around me. "Thank you for the gift, Drew. I love it."

There are no words. A simple "you're welcome" won't suffice. The necklace is such a small thing, incomparable to all the things I want to give her, but I'm glad it's made her happy.

I've spent years of my life watching those big eyes sadden from afar. Knowing my asshole of a father was largely responsible.

Lexi tilts her head back, letting me see her eyes, shining exactly like I need them to—*happily*. Her hands slide down, smoothing over the gray t-shirt I'm wearing. An innocent move on her part, I know this.

My skin flares, my cock growing hard again, every cell responding to that touch.

I want to fuck. I want to come.

With her.

Thrusting into her savagely, her wet tight pussy squeezing the come right out of me, the scent of all that wetness so deep in me that it'll become all I can smell and taste.

Jesus.

I don't even want to try with any other girl. My mind is fixated on how fucking amazing it'd be to have her.

Knowing that I can't aggravates the hell out of me. I will, someday, but until that day comes, I need to keep my distance. Being this close to her is too much of a tease.

I start to move back.

Her hands fist around my shirt.

Lexi's refusal to let me go scatters every single thought in my head, leaving only the haze.

I swear to God my vision's tunneling. That's how hot she makes me.

My shaking hands wrap tightly around her fists.

She tightens her hold before I can remove them. "Andrew . . . I shouldn't."

"What?" The heat in her eyes confuses me—turns me on more. I want her legs shaking on either side of my head. Her body wrapped around every inch of mine. It's all I can think about.

Her little hands are wrapped so tightly around my shirt that I'll have to use force to remove them.

And I fucking love it.

Subconsciously, I know what she's about to do, seconds before she does it.

Logic tells me to move back. Break her hold and put some distance between us before she comes at me.

I don't want her to be the girl I cheated on Kaylee with—one of many.

I want Lexi to be so much more than that.

My body doesn't care.

In this moment, neither does her.

I have a split second to react. See her standing on her tiptoes. Feel her little hand wrap around the back of my neck to pull my head down.

A split second where I could've stopped her.

Hell, no. I let her.

I'm too fucking starved to deny her, although I know we'll probably end up hating ourselves once it's over.

Her tongue comes out to play with mine. Wet. Delicious. Anxious.

I respond to her desperation like I've been trained to, every nerve igniting with full force.

Letting go of her shoulders, I slide my hands down the sexy curve of her back, groaning into our kiss. My hands latch onto her ass, squeezing tight.

She moans into my mouth, pressing closer.

God, my dick is so freaking hard. I nibble her lip and open my eyes—hers are already open, heavy-lidded, watching me.

Ah, shit. I lock eyes with her and an orgasm trembles through my cock. "Lexi," I pant her name, my chest heaving. "You gotta stop now, baby, or—"

She presses her hands to my shoulders and begins leading me backwards. "I want it, Drew."

12
7 YEARS AGO

Morality can be one hell of a strong driving force. It can push you out of the driver's seat, take complete control of the steering wheel and hijack the GPS that decides in which direction your life is going to go.

But it's nothing—absolutely *nothing*—when pitted against desire. Especially one that's been fed for years, an ache that's grown stronger every second it was denied what it wants.

Lexi is that for me. The ideal. The unattainable fantasy that's finally being attained.

She leads me straight back to the couch and I let her. There's no choice but to allow her. She's gripping that steering wheel tight in her hands.

I have no clue where she's taking this—me—but I'll let her do whatever she wants with me.

I'm hers.

She might as well have one hand wrapped around my cock as she leads me; that's how absolute her control over me is right now.

I should be worried over how easily she's grabbed control of me.

I'm not. As long as her hands are on me, anywhere, that's all that matters to me.

The back of my legs hit the couch. She pushes down on my shoulders. I fall onto it, eyes on her. My hands itch to reach for her, feel that ass again. I fist them, almost shaking with the effort of keeping my self-control engaged.

I've never done drugs, but I'm sure this is what the craving is like. The hunger that carves out little pieces of your soul.

I let her see it, all of it, even as I fight with myself to remain seated and let her do this at her own pace.

When she urges me to sit back on the couch and sits sideways on my lap, a low sound of desperation breaks out of me.

"Is this okay?" she whispers in that sexy voice of hers, her perfect ass perched on my lap, her eyes on mine, wide and questioning behind those glasses.

I snap.

One hand slides around the back of her neck. The other clamps down around her exposed thigh.

I have her in my hands. Right where I fucking want her.

She launches herself at me at the same time I move toward her, and then it's just our lips—touching. Meshing. Sucking. She lets me play slowly with her tongue, even though I sense the impatience mounting within her.

I press harder, rubbing her tongue with mine roughly. Caressing the side of her neck gently, I swallow every whimper she gives me. Every moan. The hand around her thigh twitches, aching to move closer to the one thing I want the most in the world right now.

I bite down on the mad urge. Control is essential right now. Beyond necessary. One wrong move, and I'll have her under me, my cock eight inches deep inside her.

Lexi rips her lips away from mine, gasping my name in a needy tone that nearly ruins me. Her hips move restlessly on my thigh.

I hiss, clenching my teeth.

Then she goes for my neck, latching onto it, all lips, teeth, and tongue, and I forget all about self-control.

I've been kissed, sucked, and tongued by so many girls. I could never count them. Almost every inch of my body.

40

But if you asked me right now what those girls felt like, I wouldn't be able to tell you jack-shit about it. I don't remember.

She bites on my jugular, moaning around my skin, and oh . . . *fuck*. I can't take it. Can't deal.

I palm the back of her head, tilting my own to offer her more of my neck. "Bite. Harder," I growl, the hand on her thigh bringing her closer. Right onto my cock.

My hips churn desperately, rubbing it into her.

Lexi sucks on me. *Hard*. Like she's trying to leave a mark on me.

God. I'm going to cream my basketball shorts. "Baby . . . what are you doing to me?"

"Drew, I want—" her voices breaks off on another moan.

Me. My girl wants me.

Rising, I deposit Lexi on the couch, her head against the armrest. One knee braced on the couch, I lean over her, breathing hard.

From the moment we first became friends all those years ago, I've been fixated on that hair. Her eyes.

They watch me now, heavy-lidded, desire hot inside those gray depths. Her big curls all over the place, framing that pretty face of hers, falling down over her shoulders and around her breasts.

The rapid rise and fall of her chest turns me on even more, and I know my cock's clearly visible through the thin material of my basketball shorts. I want her eyes on it. Her hands. Her lips. That perfect, wet tongue.

As if sensing my thoughts, her eyes drop down, widening when they land on my engorged dick.

I thumb her bottom lip, pressing into it. Probably harder than I should, but I'm barely controlling myself. It's like she's in my fucking blood, a scorching, violent hum I can't fight.

I won't be able to be gentle with her.

I shouldn't touch her like that. Shouldn't run the risk of fucking her, until I'm balls deep, like a crazed, violent brute.

There's no stopping myself.

Parting her lips, I slide my thumb into her, skimming across her bottom teeth. "You want me, baby?"

Her enthusiastic nod is so fucking cute.

"You want my cock?"

She arches, moaning.

My jaw pulses. My teeth grind together.

My heart, the stupid bastard, feels like it rotates inside my chest, kicking, kicking, demanding I fall on her and make her mine.

I slide my thumb, moist from her mouth, along her jaw. "You wet for me?"

A blush explodes beneath her cheeks, but she nods at me and bites her lip shyly.

I groan, feeling my balls tighten. How heavy they are. I don't need to look down to know there's a wet spot on my shorts, right where my tip is. "I'm wet for you, too."

Her eyes drop right back down, zeroing in and making my dick pulse toward her.

I almost jump when her hand lands on my thigh, above my knee, right where my basketball shorts end. Slowly, she begins sliding it upwards.

"Lexi," I growl out, my thighs trembling harder the closer she gets to my dick. "If you touch it, there's no stopping this."

Her eyes flash. "You better not stop."

"Are you a virgin?"

Her hand stops midway up my thigh. She doesn't answer.

I fight back the desperate need to thrust my hips at her, get her hand where I need it.

"Lexi," I say slowly, because I'm almost one-hundred percent sure that her answer might just drive me mad. "Are you?"

More silence from her.

Come on Lexi, don't do this to me . . .

"Does it matter?" she asks.

I jerk my head in a pathetic semblance of a nod. It matters. It matters so much that even I realize what a fucking hypocrite that

42

makes me, but I've waited so long to have her—claim her—that just thinking that someone else beat me to it pisses me the hell off.

"I am."

A breath of air whooshes out of me. Relief. So much of it that I'm almost lightheaded. *Mine*. "Good. I can't have sex with you tonight, though."

Her mouth opens and I see the protest forming before she even speaks.

Sliding my thigh between her legs, I lower myself onto her. "Don't worry, baby. I'm still going to take care of you."

13
PRESENT

I slam my hand onto the scanner and rush out of the lab as soon as the doors slide open. The world around me threatens to spin.

I don't stop.

Can't.

My entire life got wrecked by the centrifugal force of losing one girl.

It happened without my knowing it. It happened way before I could comprehend it. After years of analyzing the sick, twisted obsession in my veins, I realized it happened the very first time I laid eyes on her.

First day of Kindergarten.

That girl became the entire world to me. Fuck that, the center of my universe. Without her, I was thrown completely out of orbit.

I should've found another reason to go on, another reason to live. I couldn't.

It's impossible. I lived for her back then; I live for her now.

And she's here, in my building, working for my company, her presence pulling me toward her, right back into my proper orbit.

"Drew!"

My uncle.

As far as I know, he never knew what Lexi had come to mean to me. He knows I self-destructed at one point, but not the real reason why.

Anger sparks regardless. For the last two days, he's been raving about the new IT girl, and how he stole her away from Menahan— I freeze, unseeing. Disbelieving.

Lexi had been working for Stephen? *Stephen*? One of the bastards responsible for hurting her.

My uncle catches up to me. "Andrew."

I whirl on him. "Did you know who she is when you hired her?" I sound as obsessed as I am. Probably look it, too.

There's astonishment in my uncle's dark eyes, as well as that analytical gleam I've come to know so well. Like he's putting the pieces together and realizing what my reaction's really about. "I know you know her since you were kids."

Know her? I fucking *breathe* for the girl. Closing my eyes, I fight to resist the pull of her presence. I don't know what I'm going to do the moment I see her. If I'll be able to control myself.

I need some answers first.

"She was working for Stephen?"

My uncle hesitates. Most likely has to do with the fact that I haven't opened my eyes and I've lost control of my inner psycho. "Yes. For years we heard rumors of his 'hidden asset', the person responsible for giving his company such a huge technological edge."

Lexi was always a genius. Beyond brilliant. "Why was she working for Stephen?" I almost can't accept this fact. Don't want to.

All these years of searching for her, *dying* for her, and she'd been with Stephen of all people.

Rage burns through my veins.

"I don't know, Andrew. That's something you'll have to ask her," my uncle says.

Oh, I plan to. "How long was she working for him?"

45

"Andrew—"

"Answer. Me."

"The contract between them went into effect in 2012. It was almost ironclad. It took our legal team months to break through it, as well as some help from Ms. Berkman herself."

Like the pathetic, starving man I am, I latch onto that with every bit of strength inside me. "So she wanted to stop working for him?"

"Yes. Was desperate to get out. She has some sort of vendetta against him. She's going to make a great ally."

I've heard enough.

I have a pretty good idea where the software department is, and I'm almost sure that's where she'll be. This connection with her is like a radar, calling me to her.

My uncle grabs my shoulder, halting me. "Drew, what's going on?"

My entire being shakes with suppressed energy, all of it waiting to be unleashed on one woman. "Remember a few years ago, when I almost died because I was out driving high on heroine?"

"Yes . . ."

"She's the one. The reason I broke down, got into drugs. The reason I almost killed myself." *She's the reason I'm an unhinged asshole.*

"Dear God, Drew. I know what your father did to her father, but I didn't—"

"Where is her office?"

He points at a set of large doors with another retinal and handprint scanner.

Fifty feet down the hall, in the same direction I'd been heading.

Shrugging his hand off me, I take off, running straight for those doors.

Straight to Lexi.

14
7 YEARS AGO

"Take care of me?" Lexi asks, blinking up at me, all innocence. Enough of it that I suddenly feel like a piece of shit for what I'm about to do to her.

For a second, I contemplate slowing down. Not going so far with her tonight.

Her hands caress the back of my head, nails scratching my scalp through my short, close-cropped hair. Legs parting, she makes room for me and brings me down to her.

My body covers hers, my thigh pressed right up against the heat of her pussy.

A hiss is ripped out of me. So damn wet. Fuck.

She shifts, like she's aching for me to make her come, rubbing that sweet pussy all over my thigh. "What did you mean by 'take care of me'?"

I rock into her, loving her little gasp when I rub against her clit. My cock throbs with each rub along the top of her thigh, and I swear I can almost feel her pussy pulsating against mine.

Groaning, I drop my forehead on hers, careful not to touch her glasses. "It means I can't fuck you. I'm not taking my girl's virginity on a couch, in the back of a gym. But I'm going to make you feel good, baby. Real fucking good."

Jesus, I'm so fucking hard I probably won't last too long before I come in my shorts.

Lexi lifts her hips, sliding along my thigh again, and I moan at the feel of how wet she is. "If—if you're not going to have sex with me, what are you going to do?"

I want my mouth on her, lapping up every wet inch. I've never been big on eating out girls, but tasting her pussy would drive me wild. Undoubtedly.

Which is exactly why I can't do it to her right now.

"Do you trust me to take care of you, Lexi?"

She tilts her head back, lips brushing sweetly against mine, and whispers, "Yes."

My heart slams into my ribcage. I'm the son of the man responsible for causing her family so much pain. And, yet, she still trusts me.

Fuck. I really do love her.

"You have no idea how I feel about you," I say, looking right into her eyes.

Not giving her time to react, I lean down the rest of the way and cover her lips with mine.

I could come just sucking on her lips. And damn, she's a quick learner too, her tongue moving in just the right away to send more pleasure slicing through me.

I kiss her slowly, because she's wearing her glasses and I love them. So much that I need her to keep them on while I taste her.

She whimpers into my mouth, and I swear I can taste it. The promise of raging sex behind it. Her hips move impatiently. She's fucking my thigh, taking her pleasure from me, and she tries to kiss me harder.

Lungs tight, my cock so heavy, I somehow find the way to refuse her, keeping that kiss just as slow as before.

Because I've never wanted anything in my God forsaken life as much as I want her, and if I give into the call of her body, I'll end up slamming into her and busting my nut right here.

Lexi's breasts press against my chest. Ripping her mouth away from mine, she throws her head back, arching, groaning. "*Drew*."

God, who am I kidding? I won't make it inside her. Already too close.

I slide my hand under her, flattening it on her lower back, commanding her rhythm. Making her ride my thigh faster. "You make me so hard it hurts." Rotating my hips, I thrust into her, giving her more of my thigh, letting her feel my swollen dick.

Her throat jumps with her next moan.

Unable to resist it, I latch onto it with my teeth, tugging lightly on the side of her neck.

She cries out, right into my ear, and more precome leaks out of me.

"So good," I groan, licking and sucking on her neck feverishly.

"Drew. Oh God." Arching, she rubs her tits into my chest, her hips moving in circles.

I slip my hand between our bodies, refusing to lift myself away from her. My hands cup her breasts and a hungry, soft mewl leaves her. She moves faster, offering me everything.

The fire in my chest slams into my gut, spreading into every limb.

Infecting my fucking soul.

"Mine," I pant into her ear, tugging the top of her dress down. The sound of the straps tearing reaches me, but I don't care. Her tits are full, perfect in my hands, her nipples tight. I pinch them and she cries out for me again. "Fucking mine, baby. All of you."

"Yes. Please!"

"Yes, what?" I tongue her earlobe, imagining it's her clit, and play with her nipples at the same time. I lift my head just enough to look down at her, waiting.

Eyes anguished, she shakes her head. Our bodies grind naturally, our rhythm frantic but somehow in sync.

Like we were made to fuck each other.

Her next glide leaves a trail of her juices on my thigh.

Oh, fuck. That's for me. All for me. My shaft kicks, hungry to feel all that wetness. "Come on, Lexi." I lick both my thumbs, eyes on her. She shakes her head again, but fuck it. She doesn't have to admit it aloud. Not right now. Every moan that leaves her proves it.

I use my wet thumbs to play with her nipples, fucking her through our clothes. "I meant what I said. Mine. Whatever it takes Lexi."

"I want you so bad, Drew."

I pinch her nipples, hard, a broken groan rumbling in my chest.

"Andrew! Oh . . . you're . . . I'm coming . . . uh!" Eyes on mine, she locks up, coming like a rocket all over my thigh.

Near blind, desperate, I reach between us, searching . . . searching . . .

My hand slides between her legs, making contact with her over her panties.

Beyond wet.

Soaked.

So damn soaked that barely grazing her leaves my hand drenched.

"Fuck baby," I rasp. "I barely touched you and you squirted all over my thigh. That sweet cunt is trying to mark me, isn't it? Trying to leave your scent on me so that every girl knows I'm yours."

She jerks under me, mewling.

Without thinking, I raise my hand back up to my lips, taking my fingers into my mouth.

Time fucking stops at the first hit of her taste on my tongue.

Luscious.

Sweet.

The most addicting thing that could've ever been created.

Wild, practically snarling around my fingers, I suck them hard, needing more of that taste. Knowing it's never going to be enough.

My cock swells to the breaking point, *pounding.*

"Shit!" At the last second, I manage to pull away from her, landing on the other end of the couch. Hands shaking, I drag my cock out.

One pump of my fist, and my orgasm rides straight up my length, about to explode out the tip.

And I don't stop looking at her. I can't. This orgasm is hers, all hers. I want her to see what she's done to me.

Lexi scrambles to sit up and slaps my hand away, grabbing my cock—

My head falls back, a roar breaking loose.

She pumps my dick, milking me, making me come harder.

"Yours, Lexi," I hear my hoarse voice telling her. "All yours."

Somewhere, I either heard or read that sex is better when you actually have feelings for the person you're doing it with. I can officially say that's true. She just blew my fucking mind.

I came so hard I'm still twitching. Lexi plays with my dick. I'm too sensitive, but I can't bring myself to make her stop. I love that she's touching me. Learning me.

I reach out for her, cupping her neck. It takes a ridiculous amount of effort to lift myself and bring her head toward me, kissing her softly.

She sighs into our kiss.

"I meant what I said," I whisper against her lips. "I'm keeping you, Lexi. You're my girl now."

15
7 YEARS AGO

"I am?"

The sweet way her breath hitches when she asks me that gets to me. I nod at her, because for some reason, my throats too tight for me to speak, and kiss her pouty lips one more time.

A sound reaches my ears. What sounds like someone moving.

A soft snicker.

I rear back away from Lexi, my head flying around in the direction of the door.

The open door.

No one is there. Not that I can see.

My heart races, senses prickling.

"Andrew?"

I shush her, silently placing my index finger on her lips, and stand. Walking softly, I head toward the door, straining to listen.

And I hear it. Footsteps. Scurrying away from the door.

I jog to the door, anger rising each millisecond it takes me to get there.

Someone's here.

Someone heard my girl coming.

They probably fucking saw us!

Feeling like a wild animal, ready to tear into anyone and anything, I stop at the door, looking left and right.

No one.

No one on the left, heading toward the back door.

No one on the right, heading toward the main area of the gym.

I heard someone. I know I did.

"Baby, stay here." Jogging, I make my way down the hall and into the large main sparring area. It's dark, all the lights out. Seemingly empty.

Yeah right. This place is huge. A person can hide anywhere. It would take me forever to find them.

Still, the thought that someone heard and saw Lexi galvanizes me. I can't rest easy without at least trying to find them.

As I walk quickly around the free-weights area, my eyes straining in the dark, it occurs to me that only two people knew I'd be here—Stephen and Barnard.

Had those assholes snuck in and watched me and Lexi?

I wouldn't put it past those perverted motherfuckers.

Circling the sparring arena, I turn my heard left and right, still searching.

But I know it's futile. I know that, if anyone is in here, I won't find them that easily.

And I'm almost sure it had to be one of my best friends.

Then again, I left the back door open for Lexi and didn't lock it after she walked in.

Shit, shit, shit.

I'm a fucking moron.

I need to get her out of here.

When I head back into the office, she's still sitting on the couch, looking confused.

Adorable.

Her hands are palm-up on her lap and I see they're still covered in my come.

Sexy.

Her eyes meet mine and I reach back to yank my t-shirt over my head. Her eyes widen, pupils snapping wide, eating up every inch of my upper body.

My dick twitches toward her. Kneeling before her, I grab her hands and start cleaning them up with my shirt.

Her cheeks go pink.

My heart beats loud and beat through my body, demanding *her, her, her!* The chant is almost too loud for me to ignore.

"Andrew, your shirt."

"It's okay, baby. I have another in the car." I finish cleaning her up and bring her to her feet. Blood rushes hot and thick through my veins. I want more of her body. Her kisses. Her touch.

More time with her.

It feels like so much of it has already been wasted, even though we're just eighteen.

"Lexi . . ." I swallow thickly. "Would you consider spending the rest of your birthday with me? I want to show my girl a good time."

That blush deepens and I have to bite back a groan. "Andrew, Kaylee is your girlfriend. Not me."

"No," I snap, a little harsher than I should. "You're my girl. The one I've always wanted." The one I love. Cupping her chin, I hold her in place and bring my phone out of my shorts pocket. "As a matter of fact, I'm letting her know. Now."

Lexi watches me as I bring up Kaylee's number and start typing out a text.

Drew: It's over. I'm done. Not doing this anymore. Don't feel you. I'm feeling someone else.

It's harsh, and I'm a major dick for doing it over text, but whatever.

My girl watches me as I hit send. Then, I turn off my phone, because I don't want Kaylee or anyone trying to contact me while I'm focused on Lexi.

"I'm your man. You're my girl. Get me, baby?"

She nods, eyes sparkling.

Holy hell, can my heart calm the fuck down?

"Now, you down to ditch your friends so I can take you to do something fun?"

Biting her lips and smiling, Lexi gives me another nod.

I'm so high on her right now, triumph running through my veins. Finally. *Her*. The girl I've wanted for years. *Mine*.

I'll never let her go. Not now.

I smile at her, feeling how wide that smile is, knowing she can see I'm pathetically ecstatic. "Alright. Come on. Let's get you out of here. There's something I've been dying to show you."

STEPHEN

I can't believe it! That sneaky fucker. I knew he'd been lying about why he wanted to use uncle Luther's gym.

I knew it had to be about a girl, but fuck. Lexi Berkman. The hottest piece of ass in our school. Hottest tits, mouth. Shit, I'll bet she has a hot pussy, too.

Andrew let me have fun with Kaylee once when they'd broken up, and hadn't cared.

I contemplate asking him to let me have a piece of Lexi once he's through with her.

Bullshit. He won't. Motherfucker wants her for himself. I saw that.

Nah. He can't have her. I deserve that ass, not him. I'm going to have her.

I always get what I want. My father taught me that.

"Holy shit!" Barnard hisses as we exit the gym.

Andrew and Lexi left a minute earlier. They left in their separate cars, but I know they're going somewhere together. Because he wants to show "his girl" a good time.

Disgusting. Pussy-whipped already.

I smirk, thinking of the video on my phone. I can use this to my advantage. I know this. Just have to figure out the best way how.

My phone goes off. As soon as I see the name, I'm presented with the opportunity.

Fucking perfect.

Still smirking, I answer. "Hey Kaylee."

"Stephen, where the fuck is Andrew? Is he with you?" she screeches into the phone. "He just fucking broke up with me over text!"

My smirk spreads into a wide smile. So perfect. "I know where he was, and with who. She's the reason he's breaking up with you. How fast can you meet up to talk?"

16
PRESENT

My hand trembles, sweating as I press it into the handprint scanner. It's sweating too much. The scan fails.

My frustrated growl echoes down the hall. Eyeing the doors, I contemplate wrenching them open. The way I feel right now, I'll rip them apart. Shred right through the steel and titanium.

She's there. On the other side of those doors.

My girl.

My obsession.

The only fucking reason I've survived this long.

I swear to God, if the stupid scanner doesn't read my print this time . . .

It does.

I bend at the waist long enough to let it read my eye, promising myself to get rid of the scanner immediately. Nothing will stand between Lexi and me. Never again.

The software division is on the other side of the doors. Maybe a hundred computer stations. Even more employees.

"Berkman's office!" I bark out, loud enough that my voice echoes throughout the entire space.

No one answers. They all continue to stare at me, in shock. Many of them look scared.

"*NOW!*" I yell.

One girl points a shaking finger at a door toward the back.

I'm there in less than three seconds, practically flying, every limb shaking as the door automatically slides open.

And there she is.

Fuck.

There. She. Is.

That injury that never healed.

That infection that has been festering in my soul for almost a decade.

The wound that I pray never leaves me, even if the disease keeps on spreading.

Her.

Everything.

Her back faces me. Her body is different. More womanly, yet tighter at the same time. She's wearing a tight, black, knee-length dress and her hair's straight, held back in a long pony tail.

I'm immediately hit with a pang at the loss of her curls.

Even with the differences, my soul recognizes her, detonating a ruthless energy in my system.

I can't breathe, shaking like a fucking leaf.

I'm lightheaded, and yet so focused. Nothing else exits. All I see is her.

She finally turns.

Black, large glasses. Different yet so similar.

Those eyes.

God. I clench my firsts, my jaw. I clench everything because I'm sure my legs are about to give out on me.

I waited years for this moment. Planned it. Mapped out what I would say. What I would do. How she'd react.

All for nothing. This isn't how I imagined it. She wasn't supposed to be glaring at me like that, pouty lips turned down in a frown.

She's staring at me like . . .

She hates me.

I still love her. Every bit of her. More than before. More than I thought. More than I even imagined.

That hard, bitter expression on her face eases up for a second while her eyes rake me.

Analyzing.

For a moment, I lie to myself, telling myself that deep beyond the loathing I see, there's a small glimpse of the hunger she once felt for me.

But when she looks back at my eyes, all I see is that hate.

Lie or not, I go hard for her. Painfully so. I'm a wreck. Destroyed. Stripped down to the core of my psyche. Ground zero of the annihilation she left behind.

Lexi's brow scrunches, her expression morphing to confusion. Like she's studying my reaction. Like it's the last thing she expected.

How could it be? How can she be surprised? I know we only had one night together, but didn't I show her back then how much she meant to me?

I'm so hungry for her. I want to *consume* her. I want her to fill the fucking gaping hole she left in me.

Her lips part and her voice, cold, impersonal, finally acknowledges me. "Mr. Drevlow."

I nearly fall to my knees. That voice. Waited so long to hear it again. My breath hitches—then it's gone. One word leaves my mouth. One rough, desperate word.

"*Lexi.*"

Andrew and Lexi's story will continue in SSPT #2, the second episode in the
Systematic Siege: Provocative Tendencies
Short Story Series

About the Author

N. Isabelle Blanco was born in Queens, NY (USA). At the age of three, due to an odd fascination with studying her mother's handwriting, she began to read and write. By the time she'd reached kindergarten, she had an extensive vocabulary and her obsession with words began to bleed into every aspect of her life.

An avid reader in her teens, her fascination with Japanese anime eventually led her to the universe of fan fiction, which became her on-again, off-again hobby for the next ten years. During that time she amassed a following of fans that, by her own admission, she would never be able to live without. It was those fans who encouraged her to step beyond the fan fiction realm and try her talent in the publishing world.

N. Isabelle Blanco spends her days working as an author, web programmer, marketer, and graphic designer. That is when she isn't handling her "spawn", as she calls her son, and brainstorming with him about his future career as a comic book illustrator.

Will he take the apple from his Eve and succumb to her temptation?

Tempt

USA TODAY BESTSELLING AUTHOR

K.I. LYNN

Tempt

Copyright © K.I. Lynn

Cover image licensed by 123rf.com/ ©Konrad Bak
Cover design by N. Isabelle Blanco

Editors
Vanessa Bridges - PREMA
Marti Lynch

Publication Date: July 16, 2015
Genre: FICTION/Romance/Erotica
Copyright © 2015 K.I. Lynn
All rights reserved

Chapter One

Damned.

The same as every day for the last few weeks. I'm fucking damned the second I step onto the elevator and head to my office. Each floor that passes brings me closer to her and the reason I'm destined to burn in the pits of hell. All thanks to a singular female being.

Alyssa Lockley.

My nineteen-year-old intern who walks around like a ghostly and unearthly being. Eve—the epitome of innocence, elegance, and temptation divine. Born as a nymph, a siren, or faerie folk. Goddess and demon wrapped into one.

Demon. Sent to deliver me straight to hell for the thoughts I have about her.

I'm not even religious, yet I feel condemned.

After exiting the elevator, I walk down the hall, the hairs on the back of my neck tingling.

She's here.

Granted, I know she is—her car is parked next to mine.

"Good morning, Mr. Sampson." She steps out of her brother's office, startling me. Her sweet tone is music to my ears and fire to my cock.

Her internship with me is a favor for Cooper—my best friend and coworker.

1

As she moves to walk next to me, she's so close I can't help but breathe in her succulent scent. "Miss Lockley." *Alyssa*.

I keep up the professional front, even though I've known her for many years. A sense of propriety also helps to keep me detached.

Each weekend I hope to purge her from my senses, but it never really works. This Monday, just like all previous, proves how inane I am from the moment I see her car in the parking lot.

Our eyes meet for a brief moment before hers flutter away, a soft brown curl of hair falling over her shoulder. My gaze travels down her body. It lingers on her ass in the skin-tight skirt with its flirty hem, then moves to her shapely legs, and finally drifts down to her fuck-me heels. The perfect package; painfully sinful, leaving me aching after each brief encounter.

I wave at Cooper, who's on the phone. His warning is still clear as day—*touch my sister, and our friendship is over*. Possibly my life as well.

It was a speech I could tell he'd given often—to the entire male population of the office, in fact—but I think he saw the lust that exploded when I laid eyes on her. The darkness in me that called out to make her mine. To lock her away and keep her for myself.

The things I want to do to her aren't nice. They're dirty, hard, and animalistic.

She makes me this way. Always teasing me with that tight little body of hers, tempting me. Bending over my secretary's desk, her delicious ass right in my line of sight through my open office door. Reaching up to get a mug on a high shelf in the break room, back arching as her arm stretches up, looking just like she would if I tied her to my bed, writhing against me.

She smiles at me as we walk the few steps to my office. "Did you have a good weekend?"

You weren't there, on my cock, so no.

"Just me, myself, and Jack Daniels. Pretty boring, really."

I've never cheated on my wife. Marriage is a sacred vow that I took seriously, even if Rachel took a fucking shit all over it in the end. It may just be a burnt piece of paper now, months of fighting and negotiations killing whatever good we once had.

Not that my marital status really matters—the divorce papers were filed months ago—but it's the last thread I have to use to keep myself in check. To stop myself from grabbing her each time she enters my office and bending her over my desk. The lingering binding, however, is fruitless in keeping my gaze from devouring Alyssa, or my dick from weeping in her presence.

"That's too bad. You're too handsome to be alone at night."

I snap my head to look at her in disbelief, catching the pink of her cheeks before she turns away. My cock twitches and hardens as my mind plays fantasies. The thin thread of physical sanity I've been holding onto begins to fray, and I have to get away from her.

But I'm too intrigued to move from beside her.

Did I hear her right? "What did you say?" Maybe she's fucking with me.

Her head tucks further to her chest, the pink on her cheeks deepening.

I'm fucked. She looks mouthwateringly delicious and the danger warning flashes in my brain, but my now hard dick isn't listening. The precarious situation she's putting herself in with her words… Does she have any clue what nasty things I'll do to her?

Three weeks remain in Alyssa's internship, and I'm counting down the days, ready for her to be out of my sight. I can't take the agony of her presence any longer.

I want her.

But I can't have her.

Mumbled words escape her lips before she scurries away. I'm only able to make out "copies" and I swear a "get away" and "fool of myself."

"Goddamn cock tease." I take a deep breath, my fingers digging into the door frame of my office while I try to regain my calm. My hands are just itching to grab her, to claim her, to dirty her. I want to mark her with my teeth, lips, and come.

3

Instead, I force one foot in front of the other until I'm able to fall into my chair, effectively stopping myself before it's too late.

Through my Alyssa-induced haze, I barely hear my secretary, who is trying to garner my attention. I'm just sitting, trying to get my bearings, when her annoying voice comes over the speaker on my phone.

"Sir, your wife is on line two." Her words make me cringe, and I glare at her through my open door. "Don't shoot the messenger!" she calls from her desk as she gets up and shuts my door.

I rub my eyes and let out a harsh breath.

My *wife*.

"Not anymore," I growl out.

Wife? More like my bank account drainer and my cheating whore. After three years of marriage, the realization that I wasted four years with a woman who was a small step above scam artist, still stung.

"What?" I answer curtly into the phone.

"Oooh, sounds like someone woke up on the wrong side of the bed this morning." She snickers into my ear, her little laugh grating on my last nerve.

"I woke up still married to you, didn't I?"

"Touché," she says before continuing on with whatever manner of annoyance she's called about. "I was just calling to see how my darling husband was doing today."

"Cut the shit, Rachel. What do you want?" I'm already tired over whatever game she's trying to play today.

"Well, I seem to have maxed out my credit card, and I need you to call them and extend my credit line."

I'm seeing red, violent red against my eyelids that are screwed shut so tight they hurt.

"Rachel, we're getting divorced. Pay it yourself."

She makes a little *tsk* sound. "Part of the agreement is that you continue to pay my bills until it's finalized, pooky."

4

I mash my teeth together, forcing myself not to go off again. I need her to settle this shit and sign the damn papers.

"I paid the bill two weeks ago, and you are fucking telling me you spent five thousand dollars in that time!" The vein in my forehead is throbbing. "What the fuck did you buy?"

"I didn't buy that much."

"And you've already reached your limit?"

"So?"

"No," I manage to say through my painfully clenched teeth.

"No, what?"

"I'm not calling them."

She's silent for a moment, and I pray it's the end. "I can come over and relieve some of your tension."

I flinch in disgust. "Go fuck yourself. I'm not interested in your disease-ridden pussy."

Her frustrated breath comes through the line. "You fucking bastard!" she screams. "I need the fucking money."

"Then get a fucking job!" I slam the receiver down, then pick up the phone and its base and bang it on the desk a few times in frustration before tossing it down.

I slump back in my chair and rub circles on my temples, trying to rein my anger in. We eloped, which turned out to be the worst mistake of my life. We were happy for a little while, but then her true nature came out.

The one smart thing I did when we got married was to make certain she had no access to any of my accounts. I gave her a credit card, in her name, with a limit she soon pushed and repeatedly abused.

In an effort to forget about the two infuriating women in my life and gain focus on work, I pull out one of our largest client's files. I have a meeting tomorrow morning I need to prepare for.

Chapter Two

"Fuck." After almost an hour of poring over documents, checking spreadsheets, and staring at the computer, my eyes are glazed over and burning. My hands rub at my temples as I close my eyes.

A knock at the door draws my attention away from the pounding in my head, moving it down to my dick when I look up to see Alyssa peeking in.

She never says much—a quiet one—but there is such intelligence and maturity to her words when she does that I often forget how young she is. Then again, she is very smart, graduating high school a year early.

"Sorry to disturb you, sir," she apologizes as she enters, closing the door behind her.

Sir. Fuck me. It won't be long until the last fraying thread snaps, if she keeps that up. My mind is turning her respect into a depraved fantasy. Her hips sway in a hypnotic way as she walks toward me, and I can't help staring at the slight jiggle of her tits.

Shoot me now.

"Mr. Sampson, you look tense." Her large blue eyes are full of concern.

Of course I'm fucking tense. You just made my cock a fucking steel pole that wants nothing more than to make you scream my name.

6

And my *wife* is asking to ride it for money like a common prostitute. Gee, which one should I pick?

Her seductive body walks around to stand behind my chair, her hands resting on my shoulders before digging in.

"Oh, fuck." I moan in appreciation for the combination of pain and pleasure she gives me. I know I'm tense, but I didn't realize how much so until she began.

"Does that feel good?" Her voice is merely a whisper at my ear, her hot breath on my neck.

"Mmm, yes. Harder," I groan as my eyes slip closed. I'm loving the feeling of her hands on me, my mind running away with the part of my anatomy I really want them to be massaging.

"Isn't that what *I'm* supposed to be begging for?" Her overly seductive tone makes my eyes fly open.

Stunned, I grab her hands without thinking, halting her movements, and pull her in front of me. Her bottom lip is trapped between her teeth. The demon is showing through, the little bit of naughty in my innocent-looking temptation.

"Miss Lockley," I begin, clearing my throat as I adjust my position to try and hide the bulge that she creates, "that sounded like a proposition of sorts. Do I need to remind you I'm not only fourteen years older than you, but also your boss?"

My hands are aching to grab hold of her. She doesn't understand what she does to me, and her little show has me ready to push her up against the window so everyone who passes by can see *my* cock disappear between her thighs. Pink spreads across her cheeks and down her chest. I'm seconds away from pinning her down like a wild beast—an idea which excites me to no end.

"I'm sorry, Mr. Sampson, I was just trying to lighten your mood," she says, and for some reason, her response rubs me the wrong way.

I stand, upset now that she's played with me, and not in the way I want her to. Her body moves back to give me space, but my hand shoots out and grabs her arm, pulling her to me.

7

"It's not nice to tease a man like that," I say harshly. "We're not like the boys you're used to. It angers us, and many will go ahead and take what you're offering." I lean forward and run my nose up her neck, resisting the urge to taste her. My lips are so close to her ear as I whisper, "Don't tempt me anymore, Alyssa, or you may regret it." To make sure she gets the point, I caress up and down her arms, my lips ghosting across the delicate curve of her neck.

A gasp escapes her plump lips while her hand clutches hold of my lapel. "Dean."

Fuck. The way she says my name is torture. She feels so good in my arms that I don't think I can stop myself, and I find my lips trailing along her jaw toward her luscious mouth.

I press my lips to hers, doing what I've wanted to for over a month, since she first sauntered in here. My tongue pushes into her mouth, tasting her. She's fucking divine, and I lose it, turning her and pushing her against the edge of my desk.

My hips rock against her, showing her just what she's doing to me when my hard cock digs into her stomach.

I want her.

I have to have her.

A strong knock on my door makes me freeze.

"Dean, you got a minute?" Cooper calls.

My blood runs cold. "Fuck." In a frantic I-have-to-hide-her move, I grab Alyssa's arm and push her down to the space under my desk and sit down. The click and thump of the door opening makes her eyes wide as she looks up at me, but she remains silent as I move the chair forward.

"Come on in." I smooth my hair with one hand while the other pulls open the file cabinet next to me in an attempt to look like I am doing something constructive. The open drawer also hides Alyssa's form better.

Cooper's brown hair, the same shade as Alyssa's, pops through the entry. "Hey, you wanna grab some lunch tomorrow?" He steps

8

in, the door opening all the way. "I wanted to talk about Lerner and Hobbs before we give them out pitch."

"Yeah, sure. Noon? Palomino?"

He grins because I've named his favorite restaurant. "Perfect. I'll put it on your calendar. Have a good night. Give me a call if you want to watch the game tonight. Megan is going shopping with her sister, so I'm free."

I chuckle at his exuberance and shake my head. "All right. Give me a call and we'll make a game plan."

"Later!" he says as he heads out the door. I start to scoot back, but freeze as he stops and turns back. "Have you seen Alyssa?"

Her hand grips onto my leg, making me jump, which I try to play off as adjusting in my seat. She's frozen, then I hear a soft gasp as I feel her skin on my fingers and realize I've reached down to caress her cheek.

"I haven't seen her since this morning, but if I do, I'll have her find you."

Cooper waves on his way out. "Thanks."

I slump back into my chair as soon as the door is shut again and blow out a breath, then reach up and rub my hands over my face. "What the fuck am I doing?"

My best friend's little sister. She's my best friend's little sister.

And I just hid her, like I was getting caught with my hand in the cookie jar, instead of her already having a reason, as my intern, to be in my office.

It isn't until I feel her fingers trailing up my thighs that I remember Alyssa is confined to the small space beneath me. I become hard again as she moves closer.

I have to pull away. I've already done too much.

"Stop."

"But…"

I scoot back and out of her reach. There's the sting of rejection all over her face, but I can't do anything about it. I have nothing I can offer her.

9

"I'm sorry, I can't." I can hear the defeat in my own tone. "I've already taken this way too far."

She stands up and gives a small smile that doesn't cover the tears I see forming in her eyes.

"Have a good afternoon, Mr. Sampson," she says before turning and heading for the door.

Words have left me, and I can't even respond. I know if I say something, it would be about locking the door so I could pull her back into my arms. So I pour myself back into work instead and try to push her from my mind.

"Fucking Cooper." It's his fault for bringing her in here. For leveraging our friendship to pull a friend *favor*. For shoving the most decimating temptation I've ever encountered into my life and then telling me I can't touch.

Chapter Three

I've spent all of the morning, lunch, and afternoon with my dick half hard—an aching experience that's left me in a sour mood. I can't stop thinking about her or our kiss. Her soft lips against mine along with the small moan that left her and rippled through me.

My body still begs for her, unable to come down from her high. Maybe, just maybe, if I have her, I'll be able to get rid of my obsession, but there are two problems with that. One being that I will lose my friendship with Cooper and very possibly land myself in the hospital. The other problem? I worry if I give in and have her once, I'll want more.

I'm already addicted to everything about her. A monster salivating to devour the fair maiden.

How am I going to be able to stay away for the next three weeks?

If I'm being honest, I know the answer. Just as I know if she shows up in front of me right now, I'll fuck her until we both pass out. And then I won't let go of her until somebody pries my hands off her.

She's made me into a highly unstable being.

I need to get off.

Thankfully she's not sitting at her desk when I exit and head down the hall to the bathroom. Stomping in, I'm pissed to find someone is in the stall. I contemplate going to a different floor when the door opens behind me.

I rush forward to one of the urinals and undo my pants. A hiss forces its way out of me as I grab onto my cock and pull it out. It's pure force of will to take a piss with a hard-on, and almost equally so when almost hard, but I manage it.

There is the unmistakable feeling of eyes on me, but the sound of the toilet flushing draws my attention away. Maybe if the guy who came in after me would leave, I could get in the few minutes of dick pumping I need. With a glance at the urinal next to me, I quickly realize that's not going to happen.

The eyes I felt are staring at my dick as the guy bites his lip. He looks up at me and smiles, a blush racing across his cheeks when he realizes he's been caught. I recognize him from Accounts Receivable. Hired about a year ago right out of college.

"What? Never seen one up close?"

I stuff my cock back in my pants, wincing in pain.

His eyebrow lifts, the smirk on his face nothing but flirtatious, even though he still seems a little embarrassed that I caught him. "Never one that nice."

"Sorry, it's taken."

His eyes grow wide, the blush growing. I walk past him and out the door.

Fuck her for getting me this deranged and worked up.

Dirty

I'm so lost in my thoughts that the next time I look at my clock, it's after six—time to leave. I pack up my laptop and shut everything else down. Hopefully my head will clear overnight and I'll forget how right she feels close to me. If I can just erase that, I can go back to just the painful wanting. How am I going to get through the next few weeks after tasting her?

The moment I shut the door, I stop dead in my tracks, still clutching the handle. Alyssa is standing at her desk, bending over to pick up her bag.

She lets out a gasp. "Oh, my God, Dean! You scared me."

I blink at her. She's changed—no longer in her office attire, instead gracing a pair of skin-tight jeans and some off-the-shoulder top that gives her a cute and sexy vibe at the same time. It suits her, but it also makes her look so much younger.

"Sorry." It's all I can manage to say. I let the handle go, the bolt clicking into place. "You're here late."

She walks around her desk, her sexy heels peeking out of her bag. The height they provide is lost in her flats, and I'm left tilting my head down further to look at her petite frame.

"I shrunk," she says with a small smile, seeming to read my action.

We head down the hallway together. "Pocket-size isn't a bad thing."

Her elbow connects with my ribs, and she glares up at me. "Jerk."

I smile down at her. "What kept you here so late?"

She blows out a breath and rolls her eyes. "Coop."

"Sibling problems?" I hold my hand out to keep the elevator doors from closing as she steps in.

"He's playing protective older brother and getting into my business." The corners of her mouth turn down, accentuating her annoyed look. "He still thinks I'm a little girl."

I quirk my brow at her. "Little? Yes. Girl?" My tongue sweeps across my lips. "No."

Suddenly, the elevator is a very bad place to be—a closed off space with only us.

She turns her body toward me. "No, I'm not."

The atmosphere is heavy. My hands clench into fists to stop from reaching out to her. I clear my throat as the doors open and

13

step out, once again making sure they stay open for her to walk through.

"You changed clothes," I say to fill the awkward, strained air.

She nods. "Yeah, I'm going out with some friends."

We walk out to the parking garage, the sun still shining through the slats of concrete, and I pull out my keys. "Have fun."

She stands on her tiptoes and her soft lips press against my cheek. "Thank you for walking me out."

My jaw locks, and I nod. I make sure she gets in her car and is off before jumping in my own. I slam back against the head rest a few times. The spot of her kiss still tingles, sending pulsing shocks down to my balls and up my shaft. Every part of me is tense, and I have to shake my fingers out to get the blood flowing in them again from the harsh clench I had them in.

With a turn of the key I'm off, peeling out of the parking lot and getting my ass home so I can get off. But I'm left alone with myself and my actions on the drive home.

"I need to pull a friend favor," Cooper said one day at lunch. "Sure."

Cooper had dropped everything more than once to help me out, so I didn't even wait to hear what it was before accepting.

"Alyssa needs an internship this summer, and it looks better if it's not with a family member."

Over the years, I'd seen Alyssa a dozen times or so but heard about her on a regular basis. She's eleven years younger than Cooper. He and his younger brother, Damian, are every bit the definition of protective, older brothers. The last time I'd seen her was a few years back and she very much looked like a little girl.

Well, not little, but definitely nowhere near how she looked when I saw her again six weeks ago. Walking into my office to find a gorgeous *woman* had my dick's attention in a fraction of a second. The glare from Cooper as he reintroduced us though, spoke volumes.

I can't help but palm my crotch at the memory of how she looked. Every naughty secretary fantasy I'd ever had popped into my head and I was ready to enact them with her.

That night at the bar, I learned just how fucked I was.

"My little sister isn't some piece of pussy or a rebound girl." He slammed his bottle down on the bar. *"She's a motherfucking princess, and any motherfucker who goes near her better fucking treat her that way. And if they don't, they're gonna find themselves six feet fucking under. I don't give a motherfucking shit who they are."* He leaned in and sneered at me. *"Even you."*

He was a few drinks in at the time, but there was clarity in his eyes for the last bit as he stared at me.

I understand why they're so protective, I've heard the story many times, from different family members. Alyssa almost died. When she was six, their car was T-boned, the brunt of the force hitting where she was sitting. The rest of the family, minus their father who wasn't with them, escaped with minor injuries. Damian was the worst of the rest with a broken collar bone, but Alyssa had internal bleeding and a cracked skull. She was in a coma for a week. When she was finally released and her parents were forced back to work, her teenage brothers took on the responsibility of her care.

Cooper and Damian, who were already her protectors, became fierce in their duty.

Cooper warned me. *Threatened* me. He'll pummel me if he finds out how I touched her today.

To lose his friendship would be devastating. He's been my best friend since we met at Holland Finance seven years ago. He was there for me when my father died—a heart attack. Picked me up after that when I was lost. When I got married, he stood beside me. As well as through said marriage, and helping me get divorced.

Yet, I can't keep my hands off Alyssa. I may not have committed the act that would seal the fate of my friendship, but I want to.

15

What the fuck am I going to do?

Apparently I'm going to palm my cock the entire drive home.

Fuck Cooper. I'm going to fantasize about his sister and bust my ever loving blue nuts all over the place.

Two days later, I leave my last meeting of the day. It's been another day of avoiding her—Alyssa.

Monday was such a disaster, such a huge mistake. A wonderful, sinful, skin-crawling, make-me-dying-for-more day that shouldn't have happened and that can't ever happen again.

When I get home, the house is empty, quiet. I bought it before I met Rachel, so she has no claim on it.

I open the fridge and stare at the half-dozen take-out containers—cooking has taken a backseat lately. I pull out one container and sniff it, then pull back in disgust, holding it out as I walk to the trash and toss it in.

Looks like cooking is going to make a comeback.

Second time's a charm, so after a quick reheat I fall down on the couch with the remote in hand. I catch the last story on the local news before switching over for an episode of *Pawn Stars*. When that is done, as well as my leftover chicken parmesan, I head to my office with the stack of today's mail. I rifle through, tossing the junk as I move the mouse, waking my computer up.

Between work and avoiding being alone with Alyssa, the last few days have been beyond stressful. Thankfully, there's only one more day until the weekend, until I get a break from seeing her.

A quick check of my personal email reveals an email from my mom, going into detail about the events of the cruise she and my sister, Emmy, just returned from. I make a mental note to call them both in the next few days, then pull up Facebook to check in and make sure the world didn't end.

My timeline is filled with happy families and kids of people I knew in high school or college, along with a few I've met in my professional career. My own profile hasn't been updated in weeks…months, even. What's there to say? I'm going through a shitty divorce and want to fuck my intern? Two things I don't really want on social media.

I'm not on five minutes when a personal message pops up.

Alyssa – Why are you avoiding me?

I stare at the screen trying to figure out how to respond. How do I explain?

Alyssa – Dean, I'm not naïve or too young to understand, so don't even.

Is she reading my mind now?

Dean – I can't kiss you again.

Alyssa – Why?

Dean – Because I want more, and I won't be able to stop again.

Heartbeats and clock ticks turn silence into a deafening ringing. A resounding thud accompanies it with each blink of the cursor, followed by the telltale symbol indicating that she's writing.

Alyssa – Do you remember the first time we met?

Of course. That's why I can't.

Dean – I came over to help Cooper move out. You were about twelve or thirteen.

Alyssa – You were my first crush. It started that day.

Fuck, I like hearing that. At the same time, that's not where I need this conversation to go. Where else would it go, though? It needs to stop. I don't want to know.

My anger at her flares.

Dean – What is this to you, then? An itch to scratch? Satisfying some adolescent curiosity?

Alyssa – Yes and No.

Dean – I don't play games, Aly.

17

Alyssa – I'm not playing any. I know I'm a lot younger than you, but I'm also not stupid.

I know she isn't. Expressions such as "good head on her shoulders" and "mature beyond her years" very much apply to her. She's not some flighty girl. She's ambitious, driven…characteristics that keep her coming even when I push her away.

Dean – I know.

Alyssa – Do you? I'm serious, Dean. I've gotten to know a lot about you this summer, forming a person to overshadow my fantasy, and I like it. I want you for more than a scratch.

I sit back and rub my hands over my face. This is bad. Very bad.

Alyssa – Do you read me? I. Want. You. All of you.

I groan as I type out the exact opposite of what every part of me wants to.

Rationality is my downfall. Thinking with my head instead of my heart…or my cock.

Dean – I can't. For so many reasons.

Alyssa – And what are those? Cooper?

Dean – He's one. I want you, too. I want to fuck you. I want my cock buried so deep in you. But then what? We have sex, maybe more than once, and then the consequences. I lose my friendship and wreck my work life. We find out it's nothing more than physical, because, after all, I'm so much older than you. And that right there is a huge reason. Our lives are in completely different places. Do I ruin everything I've built for some pussy? No.

Alyssa – I'm not some flirty bitch manipulator. I'm not fucking Rachel, asshole.

I cringe back as she hits another root of my issues.

Alyssa – She's the bitch that would use her looks to start a war. Men have done it.

Dean – And I'm one of them. Going through divorce has taught me a lot, and to not think with your dick is the biggest lesson.

She's quiet for a moment, and I wonder if I've finally gotten through to her.

Alyssa – A few years ago you came over for a summer party at my parents'.

Now where is she going? My brow scrunches as I search my memory.

Alyssa – I was seventeen. You were there without Rachel. For two hours straight, you and I sat on the deck talking.

As the day shoots back into my mind, I recall the girl of that time who was a fresh-faced teenager. I'd been amazed that she'd just finished her first year of college at such as young age. At one point, I remember forgetting that she was so young, getting comfortable, laughing. We'd talked about where she was going in school, and she'd been fascinated with the details of accounting.

And for those two hours, I never mentioned my wife. Hadn't even thought about her. Not once.

Christ, did Alyssa have that much power over me, even back then?

Alyssa – Are you so unwilling to take a chance? We can do it in secret, no one has to know, and see. Test us out.

In secret?

It's tempting…

But how do I agree without giving in?

Chapter Four

The night was a disaster. All night, Alyssa's words, her pleading, played on repeat in my brain.

I'm so tired the next morning, I'm not sure how I drove myself to work, but I quickly wake up when I see Alyssa in the parking lot. She's wearing a frilly little flirty skirt and has a male intern paying her too much attention. I glare at her from across the way, and she jumps when her eyes meet mine.

I walk across the pavement and can't seem to stop glaring at the child ogling her.

Alyssa is smiling at him, chatting with him like she's interested.

My teeth grind together, and I grip my laptop bag tightly as my gait picks up. I have to get out of here before I smash his skull in with my bag.

I bypass my secretary and don't even bother with a cursory nod to acknowledge her morning greeting. But before I can get inside my office and hide away in my cave, Alyssa walks up behind me and says hello.

I exhale a tight breath, turn around, and glower at her. She leans back, her eyes popping wide.

Without thought, I grab her arm and pull her into my office. Our bodies are so close that she's pressed against the wall with only a few small inches separating us as every sense of propriety flies away. The moment I touch her, jealousy boils, begging to taint her more. I pause, closing my eyes before I speak to give myself a moment, rather than exploding in a rage at her.

"Do you like that boy?" I hiss and open my eyes so I can study her for the truth when she answers me.

"Hugh?" She looks confused for a moment, then the crease in her brow melts as a smile grows. "He's nice, but he's not what I want."

"What *do* you want?"

I'm desperate for her answer. Why am I stoking this fire? Stupid jealousy is going to undo me, because I'm about to snap and claim her like an animal all over my office.

There's a sparkle in her eyes, and I know she sees through me. She knows she's won. "You."

Her seductive tone sends a sparks rolling through me, and I can't hold back anymore. I take her hand and place it on my hard cock, running it up and down as I press her into the wall. An almost feral groan rips out of my chest and I lean forward, my tongue licking up her neck, making her shiver in my arms.

"Feel what you do to me. I've been hard since last night. I can't take it. I *need* this. God, I have to... have to..." Cooper's voice rings out down the hall, and I know I'm out of time. "You better come and rectify my situation today, since *you* are to blame."

I smile and step back, releasing her. She watches as I move to sit behind my desk. I'm pleased to look up and find her eyes clouded, tongue peeking out to wet her plump lips.

"So, what is it you're studying in school again?" I ask, just as Cooper's shadow hits my open door.

She blinks for a moment, stunned and a bit confused, her mouth opening and closing. "Umm, I want to be a statistician."

I smirk at the effect I've had on her. She can't even remember she's an accounting major on her way to an MBA. It makes me smile harder.

"I still think you should use your superior brain to be a lawyer," Cooper says as he turns to lean on the door jamb. "She's so good at arguing."

My seductress rolls her eyes at him and lets out a huff. Apparently it's a sore spot.

"Coop, I've told you, I don't want to be a lawyer!"

"All right, all right." Cooper smirks. "I'm just afraid of the boring stiff you'll bring home one day."

I freeze and stare at him, but he doesn't notice, still razzing on his sister.

"You do know you work in the same field, right?" Alyssa fires back.

"Yeah."

She steps forward and narrows her gaze on him while poking him in the chest. "Boring stiff." She smirks and turns toward the door.

Cooper's mouth hangs open as he follows her. "You know what, little sis? You're mean."

She lets out a giggle. "Oh, come on. You walked right into that one!"

I shake my head, turning my attention away from the retreating beauty and back to my desk. There's a Post-it note from my secretary reminding me of my early morning meeting. Not in the mood. Grumbling, I adjust my hard-on and pull out their file to get started.

Something has changed inside me—a release. The extreme tension strangling me is waking something up deep inside.

I'm still stressed about Alyssa, but now I'm determined to have her.

She's mine.

I hope she's able to handle what she says she wants.

Around the lunch hour, the door to my office opens and is shut before I can even look up. Alyssa turns around and smiles at me.

"Everyone is at lunch," she says as she walks toward me.

"Everyone?"

"Well, anyone who matters." She leans down, her lips close to mine, waiting.

I reach up, sliding my hand across her cheek before cupping the back of her neck, pulling her down as I stretch up, pressing our lips together. Soft and plump, they part, letting my tongue in to taste her. She laps hers against mine and I groan, my dick getting stiffer and hungrier.

With my other hand, I reach out and grab onto her hip, using it and the hand tangled in her hair to guide her forward. She reaches out, using my shoulders to help steady her as she climbs onto my lap, bunching her skirt up and straddling my legs as she settles on top of my aching-for-her dick.

"Dean," she gasps as she feels me pressing against her clit.

Invigorating kisses become soul devouring ones, and the only thing we care about is how much closer we can get.

I plant my heels on the ground and push my hips up, making her moan into my mouth.

"You want this, don't you, baby?" I thrust up and rotate my hips as I hold her down on me. "You want me to pull my cock out and slam it into that hot little pussy of yours, don't you?" My hands roam her body, squeezing and pulling her closer. She only moans, but I need more. "Answer me. Now, Miss Lockley."

"Please, Dean, please. I want you."

I growl at her response. I'm seconds away from taking her. Seconds from unzipping my pants, popping my cock out, pushing her panties aside, and shoving it into her tight little cunt.

"Are you wet for me? I bet I could slide right into you, all the way." I slip my hand under her skirt while I suck on her neck and shoulder.

My fingers slide along her panties. She's not just wet, she's soaking them.

"Fuck!"

I have to taste her. I *need* to taste her.

I stand up and take her with me, setting her down on the edge of the desk, then sit back down. My hand runs up her luscious, tempting legs, lifting one and placing it on the armrest to my left. I pull her panties to the side, exposing her shining pink folds. My little temptress is bare, and the glistening of her juices draws me in. She lets out a little squeak when my tongue hits her clit. My cock jumps, letting out some pre-come when my tongue runs along her pussy lips, finally getting the taste of her I've been dying for.

It only fuels my need for more of her. I dig in, closing my mouth on her, teasing her as much as her moans are driving me insane.

But they're too loud.

"Quiet, or I stop," I threaten.

Her eyes widen and she bites down onto her finger when I slide mine in, stifling the moans I pull from her. I want to hear her throes of passion but know it's too risky here, now. Later, she can scream to the gods when I have her writhing beneath me in my bed.

Her little hand fists into my hair, pushing me harder against her, my fingers deeper. The desk creaks as her hips move, needing more. I can feel her insides tighten around my fingers, pants of *Oh God* filling the office.

I curl my fingers up, and her eyes pop open as her back jumps off the desk. Half up, half down, her fingers knot into my shirt. Her mouth is open in the most erotic shape, eyes she's fighting from rolling back, and her thighs are quaking on either side of my head. Her breath is coming out in short little pants, her whole body tense.

"Come on, baby." I dip back down and take her clit between my teeth.

Her whole body convulses as a strangled, guttural cry erupts from her chest before she collapses back. I give a few more licks of her pussy as she comes down, savoring the flavor that is all her. My chest swells with euphoric pride in my accomplishment. Alyssa, completely spent, lies out on my desk, gasping for air.

I sit back and undo my pants, pulling my cock out. It's so red and hard, ready to burst. I run my hand down the length as I stare at her, at the pussy I want nothing more than to be buried in forever.

Languid strokes bring me to the edge, my muscles tight and flexing as I contemplate what part of her I want to come on first. Her pretty pink pussy? Her lips?

I let out a groan, and she props herself up on her elbows. She stares at the way my hand moves up and down my shaft.

I don't want to fuck her here. Not right now. I'm not sure I'd make it all the way inside before coming. Days of teasing without getting off have killed my stamina.

Plus, the screams I want her to make will scare people. Maybe later, after I've had my first fill.

She sits up and slides off the edge of the desk onto the floor in front of me, her gaze never leaving the dick in my hand. I'm about to make some lurid comment, but before I can, she leans forward, her hand above mine, tongue running along the underside.

The shock is too much and the fire, the tension explodes in thick white strands. The first hits her lips, and I'm shooting off as she opens her mouth and starts sucking down each spurt, pulling everything out. I fist her hair, shoving my hips up and cock down her throat, or at least trying to.

"Fucking fuck." I slump back down as she pulls the last from me.

She smiles, then reaches up and pulls a few tissues out to wipe her face off. I miss the droplets the moment they're gone, but remind myself I can do it all over again later. I can paint her with me, covering every sinful inch of her skin.

"What are your dinner plans?" I ask between settling breaths. My dick's been in her mouth—I should at least buy her a meal before doing it again. Plus, we can see if this thing between us even has a chance, or if this little lunchtime fling is it.

Though my still-hard dick tells me it's nowhere near done with her.

Her lips, still swollen from our kisses, form a thin line. "I'm babysitting Damian's kids, then going to a movie with some friends."

My jaw twitches in disappointment. Damian is the second-born child of the Lockley family's three, two years younger than Cooper, so I know there is no way she can back out.

I run my fingers through my hair. "Shit."

The atmosphere turns as we sit here, reality and awkwardness creeping in.

"I would skip the movie, but my friend already bought the tickets," she says, trying to fix it but only making it worse.

She could just be turned off because you came in her mouth, ass. She is young, after all, and...

I stop that thought. I have to break that way of thinking, especially if I'm really going to give us an honest try.

She stands and adjusts her skirt while I tuck my cock away.

"I'm free all weekend, though," she says, a hopeful edge to her voice.

I let out a groan. "I'm going to Cincinnati for a Reds game with my brother." We stare at each other for a minute and her mouth pops open, but I stop her from speaking. "Maybe this isn't viable."

"W-what?"

I shake my head. "Maybe this is just an infatuation."

"Dean, stop."

A knock on my door shocks us both, but before either of us can do anything, the door opens and Rachel walks in.

"Am I interrupting?" Rachel asks, looking between us, but then continues on. "Dean, honey, we need to talk."

26

I cringe at each word coming out of her mouth and turn to Alyssa, who is shooting daggers at Rachel. "Miss Lockley, we'll talk later."

She nods and forces a smile, but it doesn't cover the hurt and anger. "Yes, sir." She turns and maneuvers around Rachel, trying to avoid her and her poisonous radius, but Rachel reaches out and grabs her arm, causing me to bolt up from my seated position.

"You're Cooper's little sister, aren't you?" Rachel asks. Alyssa nods, and a smirk grows on Rachel's face as she looks Alyssa up and down, then to me. I curse internally at how Alyssa's hair is loose from however she had it styled, random strands everywhere, and her lips are still swollen, her cheeks red. "You sure have grown up, but you're still a little girl."

"Rachel! Let my intern go."

Alyssa wrenches out of her grasp and runs out.

Rachel struts over to my desk. "My, my, Dean, you've been a bad little boy."

I glare at her, all the venom I have for her growing. "What do you want?"

"Well, I was going to go over this last teeny detail in the divorce, but now that I see the little strumpet you're fucking, I think a little negotiation is in order." She leans forward, trying to look and sound seductive or smart, I'm not sure which.

I walk around my desk and to the door, opening it all the way and gesturing to it. "First, I'm not fucking Alyssa." At least not yet. "Second, even if I was, we're legally separated and I can fuck whomever I want."

"Even your best friend's baby sis?"

I flinch, as she knew I would. "My lawyer will be in contact with yours over your teeny detail."

She smirks as if she's won and saunters toward me, running her hand across my chest, then looks at me from under her lashes. "Teeny detail? Is that what I said?"

I mash my teeth together as she blows me a kiss and walks out.

27

If I wasn't screwed before, things are about to become even worse.

Chapter Five

Rachel's little stop had me on the phone with my lawyer on and off for the rest of the afternoon. What was almost an agreement had everything off the table again.

"Jesus-fucking-Christ Dean! What the fuck happened from yesterday to today?" Megan asks on our fourth call of the afternoon. "The sudden turnaround... She's acting like she has something dirty and is blackmailing you."

I shake my head, not that she can see me. "She thinks she does, but she doesn't."

Megan lets out a sigh. "At this rate, you'll be lucky to ever get rid of her."

Those words haunt me all afternoon. The shitstorm kept me busy for the rest of the day, so I was never able to talk to Alyssa again. By the time I went looking for her, she'd already left for the day.

So instead, I'm left thinking about her on my way home. Wondering if a weekend after what happened in my office could finally beat my obsession with her out of me.

My hands pull at the knot in my tie as I walk to the stairs, ready to be rid of my suit. Maybe I'll order a pizza and have a few beers, relax and try to get my life back to normal.

I groan after a few steps as the doorbell goes off, halting my climb. I contemplate ignoring it, but I know whoever it is can see me through the side windows. With a sigh, I move back down and with what I'm sure is a surly glare, throw the door open.

My jaw drops as a pair of large blue eyes stare back at me, and in an instant I know I'm officially a dead man. Standing on my front porch is my innocent little demon with her face flushed.

"Alyssa? What are you doing here? What happened to Damian and your movie?"

She shakes her head. "No."

"No?"

"My brother will get over it, my friends will as well. Everything got messed up today, but I'm not letting all that get in the way of what I want."

Fuck. No. Hearing that brings back fantasies reality had been beating back all afternoon. "Go back."

"Why?"

"Because you shouldn't be here."

She slaps her hand against my chest. "No! I should be here. I can't stand feeling like this. It took so much to break you down, and you jumped at the first excuse to put a damn wall back up."

"It needs to be there," I say, because it's the truth.

She pushes me back, stepping into my house and shutting the door behind her.

"Finish what you started." Her hands trail up my chest and wrap around my neck. "Then decide." She stretches up, her lips inches from mine. "Please."

With each passing second, I find it harder to breathe. My insides are clenching tight, my fingers flex, itching to touch her, and my heart races, but I stand firm. Every muscle is coiled tight, ready to either run away from her, or grab her and race up the stairs to my bed. I ignore the way my mouth waters as I stare at her.

Her lips are so close I can feel her breath. "I've wanted you for so long. Fantasized about you for years."

Stay...

Why can't I say it?

"Take me. Show me what it's like to be yours, even if it's just for tonight."

Her soft eyes plead with me, and I can't take any more.

"Fuck it." The darkness wins out, wanting to taint her, and I grab hold of her, pulling her into my arms and pressing my lips to hers. Without any thought at all, I lift her up and push her body up against the wall. I'm no longer in control; desire, lust, and greedy need are. My gaze is dark, intense. I'm hungry—so *hungry*—for her.

I can't stop, not now. My hands roam around her body, taking in her softness. Pressing my erection into her stomach earns me a delicious gasp.

"That's right, baby, feel what's going to be inside you. This is what you want, isn't it? This is why you're here," I growl, my teeth nipping at her neck.

It's why you won't stop fucking torturing me. You're here to ruin me.

"Yes," she pants. "Please, Dean. I need you inside me. Make me yours."

My fingers flex against her flesh, digging deep. "Fuck, baby." My teeth nip at her jaw, neck, anywhere I can find. "I'm going to fucking ruin you for any other man." I step back, grinning. "And I know the perfect place to start."

I grab her hand and pull her, running up the stairs and down the hall to the master bedroom.

My bed needs new memories.

No need to shut the door—there will be no one to give audience to here. And the thought of hearing her cries of pleasure echoing off the walls is enticing.

My hands are tearing at her clothing, pulling and twisting her sweater up over her head. I can't get her naked fast enough. It's been years since I've been this horny, dying to be inside a pussy.

"I haven't slept with Rachel in over a year, and I'm clean," I tell her as I unzip her skirt, her fingers work on ridding me of my

jacket. I need her to know that I haven't been anywhere near
Rachel.

"Me too," she replies. "I've only been with two guys before. I...
I haven't done much."

There's a nervous edge to her words, but her admission of
inexperience has me shuddering in pleasure of all that I can teach
her.

"Don't worry, I know exactly how to make you my dirty little
girl," I assure her, my teeth pulling on her bottom lip. "I'm going
to make you addicted to my cock."

She gasps at my words, but the dilation of her eyes tells me she
likes it. I smirk and test just how much she does.

"I want you begging for it, to turn you into a little slut for me
and only me," I say, pausing for her reaction.

She shudders in my arms, a small moan slipping past her
luscious lips. "Yes," she whispers.

I lean down to reward her by pulling a breast from her bra and
sucking on her nipple.

"Tell me, baby, do you want to be my cock slut? Does it turn
you on?" I push her skirt down over her hips to pool at her feet. I
grab her little mound and groan at how damp the thin cotton is. "It
does, doesn't it? Tell me you're mine."

I've officially lost it. The need to claim her, to take her and
fucking consume her like she does me takes over.

"Fuck," she curses, her hands gripping me tight while her hips
move, riding my hand. I slip under the edge of her panties,
groaning when I reach her bare, slick folds. My cock is weeping,
begging to be buried in her. I can't take much more. "Yes! I'm
yours, all fucking yours!"

I love the way she curses, my temptress, calling to my primal
side. One of my fingers slips in and she crumples against me, her
body shaking. I want her to come so badly, but I want her to come
on my cock first, so I pull my hand away. Her eyes snap to mine,

whispering pleas for me to finish her off, grabbing at me. I lick her sweet juices from my fingers, lavishing in her taste.

"Not yet, baby. I have to make you pay some way for what you've done to me over the past month."

She groans in frustration before yanking my jacket down my arms and off. "You're wearing too many clothes."

I moan when her lips find my neck, licking and sucking while her fingers undo the buttons on my shirt. It's slow, painful even, torture. She pulls my shirt out of my pants so that she can reach the remaining buttons. My breath is ragged, uneven, when her hands slip under the fabric and reach my skin.

It's my turn to shake, my chest heaving, head rolled back while her hands trail seductively up my abs to my chest. I grab her ass and pull her flush to me, rocking my hips into her. My hand rises and grabs hold of her hair, pulling her head back before attacking her lips with mine.

Hungry kisses leave me high.

"On your knees," I command in a whisper against her lips. She bites her bottom lip, uncertainty written on her face. "Have you ever sucked a cock, baby?"

"I have," she admits. "Once... I'm not good, though."

I nip at her jaw. "Oh, I know you're good after today, but I can show you how to be great," I reassure her and push on her shoulder until she kneels before me.

The sight is unbelievable, unimaginable, and highly erotic. Her plump lips are inches away from my dick. It twitches, and she wets her lips as she presses her hand against the bulge.

"Take it out." My voice is rough with the need that penetrates every part of me.

Her fingers fumble with my belt, then my zipper, then her tiny hand wraps around me, pulling my hardness out.

The head is full, burning purple, ready to burst. Her little mouth opens, and I almost come at the sight of my cock slipping between her lips. One of her hands moves up and down the length and she looks up at me, her tongue lapping at the underside.

Fucking perfection.

Her movements are a bit tentative from her lack of experience, but I'm determined to be the one to show her. My hand rests on her head, hips thrusting lightly, setting the pace. Her head bobs up and down, taking more and more with each pass, gaining confidence, but I want to see just how much she can take.

I want her to take all of me.

I want her to choke on me.

I'm that kind of asshole.

"Just a bit more, baby," I coo as I push her head down farther and flex my hips.

Her throat convulses around my head, and I feel like the floor has dropped out from beneath me. She's choking, gasping, and I pull out, saliva dripping down her chin. I let her breathe for only a second before shoving my cock back in, repeating the process.

"Relax your throat."

She tries, and the fluttering around my head has me groaning and tilting my hips. It's going to take some time to get down her throat, until her nose is pressed against my skin, but we'll get there someday. My hands hold her as deep as I can get, lost in the euphoria of her gagging around me.

Fuck, I'm a bastard right now, but looking down into her eyes, I know she's okay with it. She smiles up at me, my naughty little tease, as soon as I pop out of her mouth.

"Do you like that?"

"Yes," she replies between pants.

"Why?" I ask, perversely aroused by her response and the sexy smile she's wearing.

"Because it gives you pleasure."

Fuck, her answer slashes at me like fire. I take my cock in my hand and smack the tip against her cheek and lips, spreading my pre-come around her flawless skin.

Perfect.

"Aly, if you keep talking like that, I'm going to take everything out on you. I'll use you as my own little fuck doll."

"Then do it," she taunts.

I pull her up to her feet, grab her at the waist, and toss her onto the bed. She giggles when I pounce on top of her, but stops quickly, moaning instead when I take her nipple into my mouth, biting on it. Underneath her, my hands work on the clasp to her bra. I need her naked, open for me. As soon as it's on the floor, I slide her panties down, tossing them to join the rest of her clothing.

Fully naked, her reddened cheeks, lip pressed between her teeth, and knees together, are the picture of innocence. The need to see her pussy overpowers everything, and I push her thighs apart to look at my cock's new home. She's pink, swollen, and glistening—begging to be fucked. My fingers slide back into her soaked pussy and I thumb her clit as she thrashes against me, the sensations almost too much for her.

I pull them out and grab onto my shaft, running it along her slit. "Please, tell me you are on the fucking pill." I'm so close to pounding into her—my body tense and begging to take—but the last thing I need to come out of this tryst is a baby. Because it's only one time... right? She nods and I curse, "Thank fuck!"

I press against her opening and slide all the way into her sweet tight depths. My body jerks and shakes, the feeling of her wrapped around me has my being screaming out. The gasp that falls from her doesn't help, followed by her walls clenching around me. It's too much, the thin string of sanity leaving me, and I pull out before slamming back in.

"Fuck, you feel so fucking good," I moan as my arms wrap around her, needing her body as close as possible.

She cries out, her eyes rolling back in her head, lost in it all. The sight is euphoric bliss, knowing I caused it. I can't stop my hips from thrusting into her hard, my cock filling her. The pace picks up, my hips slamming into hers. Not gentle movements, but needy. Pounding into her, pushing her as far as I can.

I've had her on the edge twice, and she is quickly climbing back up, screaming and panting. My lips find hers, claiming them as every hard inch claims her pussy.

I ache with the need for release; it's been too long, my balls so tight and drawn up. She needs to come, to soak my dick and milk me for everything I have.

"Come on, baby," I plead.

She's so close, so I sit up and push her thighs apart, bending them so her knees are touching the bed. The new angle has her screaming so loud, I'm afraid the neighbors will hear her... and I love it. Her nails dig into my arms, her back arching off of the bed, head thrown back in ecstasy as she falls over the edge.

Her body convulses beneath me, her pussy becoming a vice as her walls clamp down and quiver around me. Everything turns white, my hips slam into hers, and I explode. My body jerks with each stream I release into her.

So good. So fucking good.

Better than my fantasies.

My hands are still pushing on her legs, and I brace myself to keep from falling on her. Sweat is dripping down my face, my chest heaving.

I pull out slowly, my eyes focused on where we are joined, and watch my come slowly leak out of her tiny opening.

"Fuck," she whispers, and I look up to find her staring at me. "You look so hot watching that."

I grin, my gaze moving back down. I've touched her, tainted her, marked her, and I want more.

"It's intoxicating." I drop down and place my lips on hers. "I've got a whole stack of take-out menus to choose from. How about some dinner before a repeat show?"

She trails her fingers down my chest, then wraps them around my cock. "We'll need some fuel to get through the night."

I take her hands in mine, pulling her up so that her chest is flush with mine.

I lean down and kiss her, all the while wondering if she is what my life has been missing.

Chapter Six

The next morning, I wake with Alyssa curled into my chest, my arms wrapped around her. Touching her skin is unavoidable—I *have* to. I lightly trail my fingers along her creamy skin. So beautiful. So soft.

She is exquisite.

And last night was unbelievable. It was the best sex this bed has seen by far. She tested not only my stamina, but how fast I could get it back up. If I was her age, I could have gone all night, coming over and over again. But being in my thirties has really slowed down the recovery time I had a decade ago. I still came, filling her and marking her three times throughout the night, and I'm standing at attention for round four.

Her hair is still wet from our shower a few hours prior, and she's sleeping soundly. I don't want to wake her, but my hard-on is raging. He knows there's a hot little honey hole inches from him. I lift my hips, rubbing against her thigh, and she doesn't move.

The animal inside me aligns with the devil on my shoulder, forming a plan. I'm helpless to stop their action as my dick begs for release.

I gently roll her over onto her back, climbing between her thighs, spreading her wide open. I lick my hand, swirling it around the head as I take my cock and line up. My other hand moves to rest on the bed by her shoulder, and I sink in.

It's a wake-up call she'll never forget.

My eyes roll back in my head as I move in her. Being that she's asleep, she's a bit dry, and the sensation sends shudders through my body, as I work my way all the way in until our hips meet. I won't last like this, the sensation is too strong, painful almost. My head rests in the crook of her neck, setting the pace, slamming into her.

Her mouth is near my ear and I hear her breath pick up, along with a soft moan that slips past her lips. She's also getting wetter.

"You like my cock inside you, don't you? Fucking pounding you," I whisper into her ear before nipping at her neck.

"Dean," she whimpers, her hands rising, clenching onto my arms.

Her eyes are open now, clouded with lust and desire. I rest my forehead against hers as my hips thrust harder. I'm so close, and so is she. I grab onto her legs, pulling them onto my shoulders, and giving me a deeper angle that I know will send her over the edge.

"Oh, fuck!" She's screaming now, cursing, my name falling from her lips in prayer. "Dean. Dean, oh, there. Shit!" She grips down, freezing and I come undone, spilling into her as her pussy clenches and throbs around me.

When the pulses subside, I collapse down onto her, her body still convulsing beneath me.

"Fuck, baby, I didn't think I was going to get you off."

She giggles. "It was a close call."

I roll off of her and she stretches, a cute little squeak coming out before curling back into my side.

A green light flashes in my peripheral, and I grab my phone from the nightstand. There's a text message from Jason, my brother.

Have to bail. Catching a flight to Denver in an hour. Work calls. – J Dogg

I set the phone back down, a smile forming on my face. "Looks like I'm free. What do you want to do this weekend?"

I freeze, realizing the significance in what I just said. She slides over, propping her head on my chest, smiling from ear to ear.

Looking at her, it suddenly doesn't matter. None of it. Only that she's with me.

Turns out one time isn't enough. I want more. I don't want her to go. I want to lock her away, naked, all weekend long.

So I will.

It's hard to go back to the office on Monday after the weekend I spent wrapped up in Alyssa's hot little body. Every whiff of her perfume or glimpse of her in my peripheral this morning stirs images of her naked body, bringing my dick to life. I'm hard and wanting, but there's no relief, leaving me in a nasty disposition by the end of the day.

Each day following is the same, unable to get her alone for even five minutes. Probably for the best, because I need to keep my cock contained before it completely ruins my life and hers.

By Friday, I'm tired and irritable and frustrated as fuck. It's difficult to have a meeting with a client—which has been non-stop all week—while my dick is trying to bust its way out of my pants. I just can't stop thinking about her; soft lips, plump breasts that fit just right in my hand, perfectly round ass, warm wet folds that suck me in, and my cock exploding inside and all over her.

Almost as if she can feel my desperation, the door opens and she slips quietly inside. Saying nothing, she approaches me, and I pull away from my desk.

"Mr. Sampson, I believe you are in need of servicing?"

Grabbing her hand, I snatch her tiny body to me, pulling her lips down to mine, kissing her fiercely as I put her hand over the hard bulge straining in my pants.

Oh God, finally. I groan.

40

"On your knees," I command, positioning her so that she's somewhat under my desk in case anyone should enter. She wastes no time getting my cock out, and I smack the head against her lips. "Open."

I'm being an asshole again, but I can't give a fuck because she's looking up at me from under her lashes, seducing my grouchy ass. Watching me as I stare at her plump lips opening and her pink tongue flick the tip of my cock. She knows what she does to me.

"Oh, fuck! That's… oh God, perfect." I breathe in pants as she wraps her lips around my head. My jaw falls open at the explosion of pleasure her mouth brings.

My heart is pounding and my breath is so ragged, I just know Cooper's going to hear me next door.

I grip the edge of my chair and tip my hips up as she takes me deep and sucks hard, just like I need. I'm lost in sensation as she toys with me, pushing me to the edge and then backing off. This continues for what feels like forever, and I love her hot little mouth wrapped around me.

"Fucking come tease," I hiss down at her, practically snarling in anger and frustration.

Her hand squeezes around my dick, painfully hard, as she removes her mouth. "Now, now, Mr. Sampson, that's no way to talk to the woman giving you head."

I let out a groan, my hips pulsing up, desperate to come. Alyssa just smiles at me, giving me a quick flick with her tongue.

"I'll make you come five times tonight if you'll just stop fucking playing with me."

"Deal," she says, her mouth enveloping me once again.

My eyes roll back, muscles bracing down.

There's a knock on the door, and I freeze as the knob turns, quickly sitting up and pulling my chair in, effectively stuffing Alyssa in the tight space.

"Have you seen Alyssa?" Cooper asks, opening my door and walking in.

Motherfucker.

The sweet sucking motion on my dick stops, and I'm about to kill someone. She lets go of me with her mouth, her hand still teasing, and I look up at her brother, forcing a blank expression on my face.

"She stopped by a few minutes ago, but I haven't seen her since then."

He didn't ask if I knew where she went, thankfully. There's no way I can tell him where she is and what she is doing. I swallow lightly at the feel of her tongue licking up the length of my shaft. She bravely takes my head back into her hot, warm mouth. My knuckles are white from gripping my chair so hard, forcing myself not to moan.

"If you see her, can you tell her I'm looking for her?"

"Sure, no problem."

He starts to shut the door, but just before I let out a sigh of relief, he opens it back up.

"Oh, one more thing. I was talking to Alyssa… Can you write her a letter of recommendation for a job well done?" he asks before adding, "I'd do it myself, but I'm her brother, and that wouldn't look the best."

Job well done?

Her tongue laps at my balls before sucking one into her mouth while she pumps my shaft.

Fuck, she was doing a *very* good job.

"Sure, no problem," I manage to say.

"Thanks, man. I'll let her know. I'm sure she'll want to thank you personally."

And I know exactly how she can show her gratitude.

I wait for the door to latch and footsteps to dissipate before leaning back in my chair to look down at my naughty girl. Her big blue eyes stare up at me while increasing the suction, earning a hiss from me.

42

"Your brother is looking for you," I say, pulling out from the desk a little so there is room for her to really work me over.

"I'm busy," she says. "He can wait." She smiles up at me before taking all of my cock in her mouth and swallowing around the tip. My eyes roll back as my head falls against the chair.

"Fuck, that…that… There are no fucking words for that."

I rest my hand on her head and flex my fingers in time with my hips. I want to grab hold of her hair and fuck her face until I am coming all over her mouth and lips. Instead, my will, sanity, and strength are tested, because she'll make me pay for it later.

I lick my lips and force my eyes open to watch my hard length slide in and out of my goddess's succulent mouth. I'm tempted to pull out my phone so I can take a video to jack off to later.

The idea of seeing my siren on the screen with her lips wrapped around my cock has me teetering on the edge, and she can tell. Her hand reaches up to massages my balls, and I explode in her mouth, my body convulsing as stream after stream is swallowed down.

When my breathing is back to normal, she opens her mouth wide and leans back on her knees. My dick twitches at the sight, knowing by her show that not a drop escaped.

"My parents aren't going to be home tonight," she says after swallowing it all down.

I let out a laugh. "It's been a while since I've heard that." I pull her up to me and kiss down her neck. "Do you want me to come over? Come over and fuck you till you have no voice from screaming so much?"

"Yes," she replies with a shaky breath. My hand trails up her leg, fingers dancing on her thigh. "Please, Dean."

"Please, what, Alyssa?" I ask, my body beginning to come back to life after the intense orgasm she pulled from me.

Her skin is flushed, eyes closed, her breath coming out in pants as her body rocks into my hand, trying to force it where she needs it. I groan at the damp cotton that meets my fingers. It's completely soaked through.

43

"Come over tonight," she says, her eyes fluttering closed as my fingers tease her clit and dip down to her opening.

"And what?"

An alluring pink covers her cheeks and she looks away, but I bring her to look at me as she speaks. "And fuck me until you're sated."

"I'll bring over dinner so we can keep our strength up," I tell her as I slip my hand away and fix my pants back up.

A whimper escapes her lips, and I kiss them before sending her back out to her brother, making her suffer until I see her that evening. After all, she made me wait.

It's not until later that day when she's been out of my sight for hours that I realize how wrong this is, and how much I simply don't care.

The three weeks I had previously wanted to fly by in order to get her away from me did. Only at the end, I didn't want her to leave.

I want to see her every day. I want to kiss her, hold her. With the end staring at me, I realize what's happened and how attached to her I've become. I don't want to let her go, so I don't.

Her skirt is bunched at her waist, panties at her ankles, while her body is bent over. She looks delicious spread out over my desk, fingers clutching the edge, knuckles white while I slide between her slick folds.

"Not a fucking sound." I threaten before slamming in, her body arching up while her pussy clenches around me. "Wouldn't want your brother to hear me fuck his precious little sister. To interrupt our fun and my little slut to leave my office the same way she walked in…needy. Pussy juicing for my cock."

I'm going to miss this, miss all the times I take her during the day, her scent saturating the confined space that I live in for over nine hours.

"Please don't stop, Dean. Fuck, *sir,* please don't." Her whispered pleas undo me, and I take her harder.

"Then shut the fuck up and let me take care of this tight little cunt of yours."

I'm sad to watch Alyssa leave on her last day, but it's also a sigh of relief. With her gone, I can concentrate on work without her temptingly delicious body walking by every day. We also won't be sneaking around the office and avoiding being caught by Cooper, which has happened more times than I dare to count.

Including right now. I can hear him talking to my secretary as I defile his little sister mere feet from him. My eyes close briefly, relishing in the feel of her surrounding me. I pick up the pace, spreading her cheeks to get a view at my favorite sight; my dick bottoming out in her sweet pussy.

"Have you seen Alyssa?" Cooper's muffled voice comes through the door.

My secretary responds, but I can't make it out because Alyssa's pussy clamps down and I have to bite onto her shoulder to keep quiet.

My little temptress has become the highlight, the sunshine, in my dreary days. She makes everything better.

"Where the fuck is that asshole?" Speaking of, I hear my darling wife outside and slam into Alyssa harder. "Do your job and call him. He can't turn me away. I'm still legally his wife!" Rachel's pissed, and that makes me happy. Even happier to hear her rant, angry, and I'm blissed out. I don't give a fuck about her, and there is a small sense of vindication that I feel with each suppressed moan that escapes Alyssa's lips.

Alyssa's hand clamps down over her mouth, and my eyes roll back as she pulses around my cock, making me slam into her harder. My fingers dig into her hips as I push and pull her along my length, so close my muscles are too tight to move. A grunt slips out as I shudder, my muscles releasing as I erupt.

My heart is hammering against my ribs as I catch my breath. I reach down and pick up my phone, snapping a few shots of my girth stretching her pussy as I pull out, then one of her open with my come sliding out.

"You made a mess again, didn't you?" she asks, feeling liquid slip from her.

I smirk at her. "Always."

I help her clean up, noticing that it's quieted down outside, and help her straighten her clothes.

"What?" she asks after a minute.

"Huh?"

"You're staring."

I run my fingers across her cheek. "You're so beautiful, how can I not?" She turns and kisses my palm. "And you were staring too."

Her mouth pops open, and she playfully slaps my stomach. "It's awe."

"Awe?"

"That you're mine." She pulls my lips down to hers.

One last kiss for me to remember in this space. Stepping back, she pulls a piece of paper from the small pocket of her skirt, places it on my desk, and walks out.

I don't know how I'll cope without her, but as I open the piece of paper with her class schedule, I think I've figured it out. More sneaking around and teasing texts. Spots of light in the dark. But they're worth it just to be with her when I can.

Today isn't the end of me and my Eve, but the beginning of our time in the garden.

Chapter Seven

"Oh, fuck, Dean!" Aly cries out as I pump in to her.

So tight, she is so fucking tight. I'm so close to letting go, I don't think I can stop from…

"Fuck!" I growl as every muscle jerks with each pulsating fire of come from my cock. I smirk at the feel of her walls fluttering around me, making the explosion that much better. After a few more shudders of my body, I collapse on top of her, my face burying into the crook of her neck.

I'm panting, my skin wet against hers as I kiss the side of her neck. She smiles and hums. I roll onto my back, bringing her with me, and she snuggles her sinful little body into mine, nuzzling my chest as we both come down. I can feel the combination of our fluids dripping from her onto me, but neither of us wants to let go to do something about it. Time is a luxury, and we don't have much.

Alyssa's phone goes off a few minutes later, and I know the sound—it's become very familiar over the last few weeks. It's the signal of the end of our time together for the day.

"Fuck," she grumbles and snuggles in deeper. My arms hold her tighter, not wanting it to end. Never wanting it to end.

With great reluctance, she peels herself away from me, holding out her hand for me to join her. We head into the bathroom that is attached to her bedroom and climb in for a quick shower. I can't keep my lips from her soft skin, and for a small moment we stand with our arms around each other, just staring.

Five minutes later we're toweling off and putting our clothes back on. Sadness is etched on her face, and I can't help but draw her back into my arms.

"Hey, I don't want to go," I remind her.

She nods against my chest, heaving a sigh. "I know," she replies. "I just hate to be away from you so much. I miss seeing you every day."

I rub soothing circles on her back and kiss the top of her head. "Let's go out to dinner tomorrow night," I suggest, and she looks up at me, a hopeful glint in her eyes.

"Really?"

We don't get to go out that often. Between both of our schedules, we've been confined to mostly stolen moments. We haven't had a date in weeks.

"There are a bunch of places to eat on or near your campus, right?" I ask.

She's beaming at the idea, nodding as she stands on the tips of her toes and smashing her lips to mine. "My last class gets out at six, and there is a great little Mexican place right off campus," she says excitedly.

"Apparently I'm not taking you out enough."

"It's statistically proven that taking a woman out ups your chances for sex," she informs me, a devious glint in her eyes.

"But I already get sex every time I see you."

She thinks on it for a moment. "Ok, ups your chances for anal sex."

I stand a little straighter. "I'll be taking you out every fucking night then." I've been trying to ease her into the idea of anal play for a few weeks now.

She giggles and takes my hand while shaking her head. We head down the stairs of her parents' house and out to her car so she can drop me back off at mine.

The truth is, we don't go out often for fear of being seen by someone we know and it getting out. There are things that need to be cleaned up before that can happen.

School started back up a week ago for Alyssa, putting my temptation away from the office for almost a month now. It's been agony without her, and everyone has suffered from the ill mood it has put me in. When I do get to see her, it is in brief, stolen moments, leaving me refreshed, but my mood goes downhill pretty fast once I am no longer in her presence.

My fingers lace with hers, and I hate that I have to let them go soon, that I have to leave her. The car pulls into the parking lot and to the backside of the building, where I moved my car as I left for the day. I crash my lips to hers, relishing her taste because it will have to last me nearly twenty-four hours.

"Have a good night, baby," I whisper against her lips and pull my body out of the car and away from her.

"Sweet dreams," she calls back.

I dip my head back in the car, kissing her again before saying, "They're always sweet. They star you."

It makes her smile and gives me a little more sunshine. Taking a deep breath, I climb into my car and start it up. She turns right out of the parking lot, while I turn left. Not even a block apart, and I miss her already.

The drive gives me time to think. It's terrible that my… Well, that was another thing—my relationship status with Alyssa. Though we've never really said anything, the label of girlfriend definitely applies.

That said, it's terrible that my girlfriend was so excited over a date. Am I that shitty of a boyfriend?

Apparently so, since I'm just now realizing what started off as a fling long ago graduated to a relationship. I know it's been a while since I was in a new relationship, but maybe I am a selfish bastard, only thinking of myself.

There are a couple of things I know Alyssa wants, and my divorce with Rachel being finalized is one of them. When that's done, we'll both feel better telling Cooper and the rest of her family about us. Maybe then we'll be able to fully explore this.

I'm tired of hiding. Tired of sneaking around. I'm not a teenager anymore, I'm an adult, and I want an adult relationship with my girlfriend...even if she is a teenager herself. Luckily I won't feel so weird about that soon—her birthday is next month.

As I pull into the driveway, I stop the car halfway up—the lights are shining out the windows on the first floor. I look up the driveway and spot Rachel's car sitting by the back door.

Motherfucker. She must've made a copy of her key before she gave it back.

I park the car and slam the door, storming in and making sure to slam that door as well.

She's standing at the counter in what I'm sure she thinks is an alluring outfit.

"Welcome home, darling," she says, a fake smile plastered on her face, a bottle of white wine in her hand as she pours it into a glass.

"Get the fuck out of my house."

I loosen my tie and open the fridge, looking for something to eat. There is little to no food sitting on the shelves, so I pull out a container and open it, sniffing the contents. I cringe and pull it out, throwing it in the trash—an all-too-common occurrence. I never did get back into cooking. Instead, I pull out a bottle of red wine and pour a glass.

She watches me, unfazed and not leaving. "I was thinking...maybe we could spend some quality time together."

"I don't want to spend any time with you, quality or other." I down half the glass, so annoyed I'm unable to even enjoy it.

"Dean," she begins, standing in front of me and placing a perfectly manicured hand that I paid for on my chest. I glare down at it, jaw clenched tight. "I feel like I hardly see you anymore.

You're always working." Her hand creeps higher, and my eyes narrow further. "Baby, why don't we move to the bedroom…?"

"What do you want?" I snap, cutting her off.

"I was just thinking we should go on vacation, maybe to Tahiti or something. Spend some time together, just the two of us. I think we need to…reconnect. Stop all this silly divorce nonsense." She reaches down and cups me, but it doesn't stir anything.

I grab her hand and pull it from my body. "Rachel, I don't want you."

She pulls back, her face screwing up into an annoyed look as she crosses her arms. "Are you sleeping with someone? Cooper's little sister? My lawyer said it doesn't matter, since there's no evidence it started before the divorce, but that's it, isn't it? That's why you won't give in?"

"I won't give in because I can't stand the thought of entering a place that countless men have been since we met," I sneer, and she gasps in indignation. "Don't try to deny it. You fuck anything with a dick."

"What the hell do you call what I'm doing now?"

"Seducing me so you can get whatever expensive thing you want today… I'm not stupid," I say and push past her, picking up my laptop and heading down the hall.

"No, you're just an idiot! I got you to marry me without a prenup!"

I stop in my tracks and turn toward her. She's smirking at me like she's won.

"That may be the case, but who has all the access to the money? Yeah, not you, bitch."

My retort wipes that damn smug look right off her face and she turns red, screeching at my back.

"I'll take you for everything, Dean! Everything!" she screams.

"Get the fuck out, Rachel, before I call the cops." I don't wait to hear her response, letting the slamming of my office door cut her off.

Slumping down in my chair, I rub my face. I was happy half an hour ago, and within five minutes of getting home, I'm miserable. I pull out my phone and send her a text, knowing she's probably made it to her evening class.

I miss you.

Simple, but it's very much the truth.

Miss you too *kisses* – Aly

I chuckle at her response and relax a bit. Just talking to her, even in this manner, calms me. Maybe it's because in the almost two months we've been together, she gets me more than Rachel ever has. Alyssa might be young, but I've never felt a connection to anyone like the one I have with her. Smart, sweet, sassy, modest, and sexy as hell.

My little temptation with her seductive, plump lips…

I smirk as I look at the clock; she's in her business lecture. The perfect opportunity to send her dirty texts.

Tomorrow I'm going to eat you out until you're begging me to stop. Then you'll wrap your luscious lips around my cock and take it all in before I fuck you until you pass out.

That should make her squirm.

It's not a moment later that my phone buzzes with her reply.

Meanie!! And I'm looking forward to dinner and the after show. ;) – Aly

I smile and put the phone away, moving instead to the large stack of mail. The bills I pull aside while the rest meets the trash can. I rub my face and open up my email, looking for anything that isn't garbage. Then I log onto Facebook for my daily dose of social media. Alyssa is in class, so I can't chat with her, but as I scan the list of people online, I stop at Megan Lockley—Cooper's wife and my divorce lawyer.

Megan is an awesome ally to have on my side, and I'm happy to have someone I know and trust handling my shit divorce. I first met her five years ago, shortly after she started dating Cooper. It was the friend *test*. That night we did shots, head-to-head, and when I won, she called me a "fucking, wanking tool." When I asked her which was it, fucking or wanking, she snorted and said "Well, you're fucking your hand when wanking it, aren't you?"

She got the thumbs up, and I can't see a more perfect woman for my best friend.

Dean: Need you.

Megan: Sure. Cooper's at the gym. What's going on?

Dean: Rachel was here when I got home. Can we use that against her so she'll finalize this damn thing? I want it over. I need it over.

Megan: Coop says you've seemed happy lately. Does that have something to do with it?

Dean: It's been a year. I'm ready to have her completely out of my life. And yes, being happy is part of it but I can't elaborate right now. Cooper will kill me when he finds out.

Megan: Unless you're fucking his sister, I don't think he'll care.

My eyes widened at the screen. It was just a flippant comment, but she hit the nail on the head. My silence must have been too much, because Megan is typing again.

Megan: Oh, God, please tell me that's not it. Please tell me you aren't banging Alyssa.

Dean: I want to be free to date her without all this baggage from Rachel.

Megan: Dean, this is serious. You're one of his closest friends. When he finds out what you've been doing...it won't be pretty.

Dean: I know, but I don't think I can live without her anymore.

My admission startles even myself. She is my temptation, my Eve, and I don't want to be apart anymore. She breathes life into me, and I want her with me always.

I want to spend forever tainting her, making her as addicted to me as I am to her.

Chapter Eight

Two weeks later, I'm on campus to pick Alyssa up. I have her class schedule memorized, texting her dirty messages during lectures, teasing her as she did me. Turnabout is fair play and alive in the replies that I receive, leaving me hot, bothered, and desperately wanting. Sometimes even while I'm meeting with clients, which can be very distracting.

I've made some changes in my life, one being putting my foot down with Rachel and the divorce. The second is making sure both me and Alyssa carve out time at least twice a week for dinner. During those few short hours I'm privileged too each week, I'm strained to cram in all of my emotions, all of my needs. It's time I've become dependent on. Dependent on seeing her, life reviving into my system and making me functional again.

My dependency has led to a jealousy and fear that I'm unable to express. For the first time in my life I have something real. Someone that I care about with my whole being. But what right do I have to be jealous? I'm a much-older-than-her, still-married man. Doubts creep in, and I'm left eviscerating myself in examination for what I have to keep her. If she leaves me for a guy closer to her age, there's nothing I can do.

If she leaves me…

One small sentence that shakes my core and shoves it in my face just how much I feel for her. What started out as a little affair, a sexual need, has grown into much more than I could conceivably imagine.

Cooper has noticed the difference in me. He thinks it's because of a woman, and he's right, but I haven't told him anything. Megan has kept her promise and is the only one that knows about us.

"Dean!" Alyssa calls out as she runs to me, her messenger bag swinging.

She jumps into my arms, making me stumble back. I chuckle at her excitement in seeing me. It calms me, knowing she missed me too. I feel the exact same way she does.

"My little temptress, I've missed you so much," I say, pulling her as close as I can, kissing the top of her head.

She laughs and shakes her head. "It's only been a day."

"And who jumped into whose arms?"

She bites her bottom lip. "The woman who's missed you so much she can't contain her happiness in seeing you."

Her words work to appease the doubts that are always circling in my brain—if I was closer in age to her, would we be together? *Could* we be together? Would we have a fighting chance?

We have many obstacles, and a future unknown.

Then it hits me...

Fuck. I've fallen in love with my temptation.

More than just unadulterated lust for her sinful body, I also want her mind and her soul. I want everything she has to offer me. And it's been this way for weeks...more like months.

"If you say things like that, I'll never be able to let you go," I whisper in her ear.

She pulls back, smiling up at me. "Then don't."

"There's so much..." I'm silenced by her fingers on my lips, her beautiful eyes staring up at me with no hint of humor.

"My brother, well... he'll just have to get over it. Honestly, I'm a little confused by you at the moment. Where is my confident, alpha guy? This Dean seems vulnerable, and I'm wondering what has caused my beautiful man such discomfort."

My eyes seal shut, my forehead resting on hers. She's never been this blunt before about us, about what she wants—what we both want. In the past few months, she seemed content to only take what I could give her in stolen moments. But now, we both need more. We need to make this something we can have all the time and around the people we care about.

"You have," I admit. "Being with you."

There is a moment of pause before she moves to step out of my arms, but I hold her tight.

"So that's it? Come to brush me off. You've had your fill then? Done with the little girl?" she asks angrily, twisting to get out of my arms, and I realize she's taken my words the wrong way. "Let go of me, Dean!"

"You misunderstood me," I say, tilting her head to look at me. Tears fill her eyes, her bottom lip trembling. "You make me vulnerable and insecure."

"How could I make you that way?" She reinvigorates her attempts to get away, but I hold her in place.

"Because I've fallen in love with you, and I'm terrified of losing you."

Her tear-filled eyes turn to look at me, disbelief written on her face. "Don't say that to appease me."

"I love you, baby, so much," I say again, solidifying my words, my forehead resting on hers.

Tears fall from her eyes, her features morphing from pain to a breathtaking, brilliant smile covering her face.

"I love you, too," she whispers before crashing her lips to mine.

I moan into her mouth, my hands grab onto her soft body, and my cock grows hard.

"Come on, let's go." I grab her bag and she wraps her hands around my arm.

Life's about to get interesting.

Dirty

"Calm down, baby, you're sweating," Alyssa says, trying to soothe me, running her fingers through my hair.

I'm walking into the lion's den. Of course I'm sweating!

It's Alyssa's birthday, and her family is having a party for her. I know we've had this planned for weeks, coming out to her family, but now that it's upon us, the reality is harder than the fantasies we'd been having.

We're here to tell them we're together, her whole family, which includes Cooper. It's one of my birthday presents to her—being free to be together.

Cooper's already here, his car in the driveway, and I'm a nervous wreck about my best friend's reaction. Alyssa slips her hand in mine, giving me a reassuring kiss, but it does little to help. Her family thinks they are meeting her boyfriend, "Adam," but they're in for a big surprise.

"Just remember, it doesn't matter what they think," she says.

I agree, but it doesn't change the level of anger I know is going to be aimed at me.

She calls out to her parents as we walk in, and I stop breathing. I've never been so nervous to meet a girlfriend's parents, although I already know hers. I even have their phone numbers, gotten drunk with her father a dozen times, and bought her mom Mother's Day cards.

Cooper's voice echoes around the walls, growing louder as we enter the open area that holds the kitchen and living room.

"Alyssa!" Cooper grins from ear to ear as he jumps from his seat on the couch and runs over. The smile dies when his eyes land on me. Confusion takes over, but when he sees her hand in mine, it all clicks and I steel myself for my punishment. "Son of a bitch!" His fist collides hard with the side of my face, sending me slamming to the floor.

There are shouts and angry words flying around, along with the ringing in my head, but the one sound that cuts through it all is Cooper falling down on the ground right beside me. I look up to find a very pissed off Alyssa glaring down at him, her fist clenched tight.

That's my girl.

"He's married, Alyssa!" Cooper protests, hand holding his jaw where she'd hit him. "And more than a decade older than you!"

I rub at my jaw and look at the crowd we've amassed. Her parents are standing around, along with half a dozen other family members, all of them wide-eyed and confused. Among them is also Damian, her other brother, who is shooting daggers at me, poised to come at me as well, until his wife, Gia, touches his arm, holding him back.

Her father is starting to turn a very deep shade of red as he glares at me. "Dean? What is going on?"

I can't even answer, because Alyssa is yelling at Cooper. "I don't care, and neither does he! We love each other. We're together, and there's nothing you can do about it!"

"He's *married*!" Cooper protests.

"Is he?" Megan strides in and over to me with a smirk. "Ah, Dean, there you are. I believe I have that present we talked about right here." Megan smiles at me while handing me a case file, a look of utter disbelief from Cooper as he looks at his wife.

Flipping it open, I'm ecstatic to see the name *Rachel Sampson* scrawled out next to the word "wife." I peel myself from the floor, Alyssa grabbing onto my arm to help, and hold out the signature page for her to read.

"Happy birthday, baby."

She reads it, her hand moving to cover her mouth as tears fill her eyes. "Really?" She looks up at me, and I nod.

The bound papers go flying and she's in my arms, kissing me, not giving a fuck who's watching.

"Will someone tell me what the hell is going on?" Dan, her father, screams in agitation.

Alyssa picks the papers up from the floor and shoves them at him, beaming. "He's divorced! Finally!" She's bouncing up and down, and back into my arms, knocking me back into a wall. "Best birthday present." Her lips are on mine, and I can't keep my hands from roaming her body.

"That's not what I'm talking about, young lady."

Alyssa slides out of my arms and grabs my hand, taking us to stand in front of her family. "You invited my boyfriend." She wraps her hands around my arm.

Everyone stares in shock at the whole situation.

Cooper picks himself off the floor and walks forward. "For months you've been fucking my sister, even after I warned you?"

"Things happen, man. I didn't want to tell you until I knew for sure it was more."

Cooper steps closer, his fists clenched. "More what? More than just fucking?"

I brace for the next hit, ready to take my punishment. "I'm sorry, Coop. I never meant to betray your trust and friendship, but—"

"Her young pussy was too tempting to stay away from?" he cuts me off.

"Cooper!" Amy, his mother, yells in disapproval. "Let him explain."

Alyssa steps between us, reading the signals coming off Cooper in waves. "Stop being an asshole!" She pushes against his chest, creating some space between us. "Yes, he's your friend and I'm your sister, but he's not using me or whatever is going through that head of yours. We're in love. Deal with it, Coop, because we're together, and you throwing a tantrum or beating him up isn't going to change that."

Cooper doesn't say anything, but he glares at me, before pushing past us as he storms out the door, slamming it hard.

Megan lets out a sigh. "Give him some time. He'll come around."

I shake my head. "I don't know about that."

"It will take a while, and probably some bribing on both your ends, but eventually."

Megan follows after him, and we turn back to the crowd only to be confronted by a disappointing look on Dan's face. "Dean, Alyssa? You're like a son to me."

"And?" I ask. "Why will that change? It's not like this was planned. I'm older than her. Trust me, I've already run through the gamut of our age difference, and in the end, Alyssa won out."

"I can't condone this," Dan says, shaking his head. "Having an affair with my daughter? She's almost young enough to be yours!"

"He's not—"

Dan points his steely glare at Alyssa. "Silence!"

Amy lets out a squeak and looks between us and her husband. "Dan, don't."

"No, Amy." Dan is ten shades deeper red in the face. "She's nineteen and lives under my roof, therefore, my rules."

Alyssa swallows and stands straighter. "We don't care what you say."

I follow her actions, tightening our front. "That's right. Kick her out. Please. My house is lonely when she's not there."

Alyssa's head snaps to me. "What?"

It's finally my turn to smile at her. "I didn't want to love you, but you made it impossible for me to resist. I'm tired of being without you all the time. Move in with me?"

"No!" Dan snaps, but Alyssa's attention is all on me.

She cups my face and pulls my forehead down to rest on hers. "You're full of surprises today. My heart…" She lets out a sigh. I reach up and swipe a falling tear from her cheek. "My heart can't contain how much I love you right now."

I run my nose along hers. "Is that a yes?"

She lets out a happy laugh. "I'd say yes to just about anything right now, but definitely to moving in."

"Don't tempt me to ask you to marry me." The words fly from me before I can stop them. It's not that I haven't thought about it, but neither of us are ready for that right now.

She stares at me, stunned, then her face morphs into that sexy smile I know all too well. "When we're ready, I'm pretty sure I can be convinced of that."

I smile at her and nuzzle her nose. "Mother of my children?"

She beams at me. "One day, that too."

"I love you," I whisper against her lips.

"Not as much as I love you."

Words that make everything worth it.

Eight Months Later...

The end of the day has finally arrived, and there's only thirty seconds remaining before five o'clock hits and I'm out the door. After shutting off my computer and stuffing my laptop into my bag, I close the door to my office and walk down the hall.

"Hey, Coop, you ready?" I ask as I tap on the door two down from mine.

His head pops up, eyes almost spinning. "The day's over?"

I chuckle and lean against the door frame. "Yup." He looks down and then back up to me, his mouth opening, but I stop him. "Shut it off. Dinner's at six."

He lets out a groan, finding something to mark his place, and shuts everything down. After packing up, he looks at me, his brow quirking up. "Why are you so happy about my dad's birthday dinner?"

A grin spreads on my face. "Finals are over."

He blows out a breath. "Thank fuck!" He starts to say something, but then catches himself. "If she wasn't my sister, I'd say something about you getting your rocks off and out of the shitty mood you've been in." Stepping around his desk, he walks out into the hall and we head to the elevator. "But, she *is* my sister, and I don't want to know any of the fucked up details about the kinky stuff you do to her."

It took Cooper about a month to warm up to me being with Alyssa, but when he saw how happy she was at Thanksgiving, he fully caved. I still got the "Hurt her and I fuck you up" speech and subsequent warning, but this time with a hug at the end.

"See you in a few." Cooper waves as he gets into his car.

I wave back and do the same to head home.

Home.

Eight months later and it's hard to remember my life without her there.

We left her birthday party with a few bags of her stuff, completing the move over the weeks that followed. There were a few ups and downs during those first months, but mostly due to getting used to each other. After everything we'd been through to have a relationship, our commitment to it and each other never faltered.

It only takes ten minutes to get home, and thirty seconds to get in the door. With each step from the garage to the door, my dick gets harder.

"Baby, I'm home!" I call out, just as I do every day.

There's no pitter-patter of feet, no "In here," no searching out my music-listening, headphone-clad love, because she's sitting on the counter in front of me. The same counter that has proven time and time again to be the perfect height for fucking.

And she's naked.

Was my dick getting hard? It's a raging boner now.

She's biting her lower lip, excitement vibrating off her as she swings her legs over the edge.

"Finals are over."

My bag is on the floor and I race to her, spreading her legs and stepping between them. I run my hands up her thighs and around her waist as I crash my lips to hers. Tasting her delicious mouth, like a man dying of thirst, I rock into her.

"How did they go?" I ask as I pull back for a breath.

"Great." She reaches between us and works my belt open. "Talk later, fuck now."

The bare minimum—pants undone, cock out—and I'm sliding in.

She's fucking heaven. It feels like years since I've felt her tight pussy around me, even though it's only been a week. But just like now, that was a quickie.

My eyes roll back as I thrust into her. She's so tight and wet. "You've been playing with yourself."

She giggles against my lips. "Time is short, and I can't wait any longer. Preparation was necessary. Just thinking of your cock…" She draws in a sharp breath as I plunge all the way into her.

"What about my cock?"

A shiver runs through her, and her eyes become cloudy. "It's fucking perfect."

With a smirk, I dig in, pushing in and pulling out with increasing speed and pressure. It doesn't take long for her hands to fist my jacket and her back to arch into me as her mouth drops open and her pussy clamps down. Spine tingling, fire-rumbling, pain-filled pleasure rips through me and I grip her hard as my cock fires off in unexpected pulses deep inside her.

"Fuck!"

With shuttering, gasping breaths, I pull back and look at the lazy smile forming on her face. She's still fluttering around me, both of us coming down.

"I think you need another all-nighter tonight," I say, watching my dick slowly slip from inside her.

"For what?"

I lean forward and smile. "Hmm, maybe Dick Sucking 101."

She wraps her arms around my shoulders and shakes her head. "That's a freshman level course. I'm officially a senior." Her lips ghost across mine, a vixen twinkle in her eye. "Maybe this weekend I could enroll in Anal 405."

My dick twitches. The magic fucking word I've been dying to hear—*anal*.

"You're cruel."

"What? Why?"

"Because we have to leave in ten minutes and all I want to do is lock you away for a week."

"We could always skip."

I chuckle. "No, it's your father's birthday, and he would not be happy with me."

A week after the birthday disaster, after things settled down, her father wanted to talk.

I sat across from him, elbows resting on my knees. "I didn't go into this lightly, Dan. I went through it all, and every objection I had, she beat down."

He let out a grunt. "She was on the debate team in high school. But why all the secrecy?"

"To find out if it was worth it," I told him, because it was the truth.

"Was it? Is it?"

My lips curled up into a smile. "Yes. If, after today, you never want to see me again. Fine. But I love Alyssa and she is staying with me. She's my responsibility now, not yours. I will take care of all her needs."

He was silent for a moment, his arms crossed in front of him. "Amy says I overreacted."

"Did you?"

He nodded. "I know you're a good man, Dean. It was such a shock to see you with her like that, to see Cooper's reaction. The surprise caught me off guard."

"You hurt her."

He nodded again. "I'll make it up to her."

He did, eventually.

"Baby, what are you wearing?" I call from the closet, staring between my suits and jeans.

She walks in and shifts through her clothes. "A sundress. Why?"

"Just trying to gauge formality."

She stands on her tip toes and places a kiss to my cheek. "Jeans and a nice shirt will be perfect."

I turn to kiss her and draw in a breath. "Fuck." She's wearing nothing but a thong, her perky tits begging me to suck on them.

"What?" she asks innocently, with a wicked gleam in her eye.

I snap her thong strap, earning me a screech. "Come on, temptation. I'll punish you later."

She throws a dress on over her head, then slips on some sandals. "I look forward to it." She wraps her arm around mine as we head out.

"All weekend long."

She quirks a brow at me. "Just the weekend?"

No, not just the weekend. I planned to have her for the rest of my life.

About the Author

K.I. Lynn is the USA Today Bestselling Author from The Bend Anthology and the Amazon Bestselling Series, Breach. She spent her life in the arts, everything from music to painting and ceramics, then to writing. Characters have always run around in her head, acting out their stories, but it wasn't until later in life she would put them to pen. It would turn out to be the one thing she was really passionate about.

Since she began posting stories online, she's garnered acclaim for her diverse stories and hard hitting writing style. Two stories and characters are never the same, her brain moving through different ideas faster than she can write them down as it also plots its quest for world domination...or cheese. Whichever is easier to obtain... Usually it's cheese.

www.ingramcontent.com/pod-product-compliance
Lightning Source LLC
Chambersburg PA
CBHW021147130626
46554CB00005B/1710